Books by Kara Lennox

In memory of my uncle, Captain Henry "Pearly" Gates, who was a Dallas firefighter for many, many years.

Her Perfect Hero
Kara Lennox

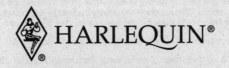

TORONTO • NEW YORK • LONDON
AMSTERDAM • PARIS • SYDNEY • HAMBURG
STOCKHOLM • ATHENS • TOKYO • MILAN • MADRID
PRAGUE • WARSAW • BUDAPEST • AUCKLAND

ISBN-13: 978-0-373-75154-9
ISBN-10:   0-373-75154-0

HER PERFECT HERO

www.eHarlequin.com

Printed in U.S.A.

Julie climbed the ladder and balanced herself precariously at the top

With a screwdriver and a hammer she tried to pry one of the ceiling tiles loose, but they'd been up there for almost a hundred years and they weren't coming down easily. Finally she managed to get the hammer's claw wedged under one corner. She pried with all her strength, but got nowhere.

The front door opened and a shaft of sunlight cut through the bar's dusty interior. A man stepped inside, silhouetted in the doorway. Julie recognized Tony's broad shoulders, his muscular chest, his dominating presence. She took a deep breath.

She started to say something—and then everything happened at once. With an earsplitting noise, the tin panel above her pulled partly free. Julie clawed at the air as she lost her balance, startled by the falling panel. She braced herself, wondering what kind of injuries she'd sustain when she landed.

But she didn't hit the floor. Instead, she fell into a strong pair of arms as perfectly and neatly as if she'd dropped into a hammock. It took her a few moments to realize she was okay.

"What are you doing here?" she asked inanely.

"Is that any way to greet a man who just saved your life?"

Dear Reader,

In the first FIREHOUSE 59 book I introduced readers to Brady's Tavern, a slightly unsavory bar across the street from the station. In *Her Perfect Hero*, my heroine, Julie, takes over Brady's. The fun starts when the firefighters get wind of her plans to give their favorite hangout an extreme makeover, and Tony gets caught in the cross fire.

I tried my best to bring Oak Cliff neighborhood to life. It's a place I love because it's my home, too. And although Brady's is fictional, I incorporated a lot of real places into the story. As for Tony, he's fictional—I only *wish* he were real. I hope you'll love him as much as I do as he struggles with his divided loyalties.

Happy reading,

Kara Lennox

Chapter One

Tony Veracruz climbed off Engine 59 pumped full of adrenaline for which there was no outlet. Around midafternoon his crew had been called to a house fire in South Dallas. But by the time they'd arrived another company had had the small blaze under control and there'd really been nothing for him to do.

Back at the station, he halted traffic on busy Jefferson Street so Lt. McCrae could back the engine into the apparatus room. He willed the alarm to buzz again, but annoyingly it remained silent.

For the past ten or so hours in the August heat he'd gone on one call after another, including the rescue of a kid stuck in a drainage ditch. All of which had, thank God, distracted him from thoughts of Daralee.

Now, with nothing to keep his brain occupied, he could think of nothing else. He wished he could banish her from his head. She was finished with him, and nothing he could do would bring her back.

For the past week, ever since their breakup, the only thing that could wipe her from his mind was the sound of that alarm.

As he followed the engine into its bay and prepared to close the door, movement across the street caught his eye.

"Hey, Ethan," he called to his fellow firefighter and lifelong best friend. "The lights are on at Brady's."

His announcement got the attention of everyone within earshot. The guys who'd been on the engine joined him in the open doorway to gaze at the illuminated beer signs in the front window of Brady's Tavern. The signs had been dark for the past two weeks, ever since Brady Keller, third-generation owner of the best bar in Dallas's Oak Cliff neighborhood, had died peacefully in his sleep.

"Maybe it's opening back up," Ethan said.

Tony shrugged. "We can only hope."

Oak Cliff had once been its own town, but Dallas had swallowed it up more than a hundred years earlier. It comprised a large area across the Trinity River from downtown and came with a diverse population and plenty of character. Those who lived and worked there tended to think of themselves as different—outside the mainstream—from other Dallasites. In turn, Dallas proper didn't think all that much of Oak Cliff.

Brady's was an Oak Cliff institution, and Tony had frequented the bar since he'd acquired his first fake ID at age seventeen. Located just across the street from the fire station, it was a favorite hangout for cops and firefighters.

And good ole Brady Keller had been as familiar a fixture as his tavern's sticky wood floors and antique shuffleboard table. He'd always been there, ready to listen, commiserate and even serve up an occasional beer on the house, provided your tale of woe was sad enough. Whenever Tony broke up with a girl—which happened with alarming frequency—he'd headed straight for Brady's, where he could distract himself with a game of pool, a sporting event on TV and a cold one. Until the bar had closed its doors.

Fire Station 59 had gone into mourning at the news of Brady's death, especially when the For Sale sign had gone up.

"Did you see who's inside?" Ethan asked.

"I think I can see someone moving around," said Priscilla Garner, another of Tony's good friends. She, Ethan and Tony had gone through firefighter training together. Now they all lived on the same block, worked the same shifts and watched each other's backs. As the three greenest rookies, they took a lot of grief from the veterans. "Maybe someone bought the place."

"I saw who went inside," said Otis Granger, who'd had a stool with his name on it at the bar. Otis hadn't gone on the last call. "Two girls, and they didn't look like bar owners to me."

"Girls?" Tony's interest immediately picked up.

"Well, women, if you want to be politically correct," Otis explained. "But one of them was a teenager, I think."

They were all hoping someone would buy the

place and open it up just as it had been. Brady's business had fallen off some in recent years as newer, trendier bars had opened in Oak Cliff, but none of his regular customers wanted to see the bar change.

"I think we should find out who they are," Ethan said. "Brady must have family—someone to inherit. He talked about a sister."

"Tony, go talk to them." Priscilla gave him a little shove.

"Why me?"

"Duh… They're female. I don't know if you've noticed, but you have a certain effect on women."

Otis and Ethan broke out laughing, but Tony didn't. Whatever effect he had, it never lasted. His longest romantic relationship had ended after only a couple of months.

"Just go find out who those women are," Priscilla urged. "They must be related to Brady somehow. Ask them what their plans are. Maybe you can impress on them how important it is to sell Brady's to someone who'll reopen it and keep things the same."

"Ethan, why don't *you* talk to them?" Tony argued. "You're the great persuader around here."

"Yeah, he managed to convince Kat to marry him," Otis said drily. "Like she couldn't have done a lot better."

Ethan puffed out his chest, as he did at any mention of his beautiful new bride. They'd been married less than a month. "Okay, I'll talk to the ladies."

Just then, the door to Brady's opened and one of the women emerged.

Even from a distance, Tony could see she was gorgeous—tall and sleek, with golden hair that blew in the breeze. She wore snug faded jeans that molded themselves to a body made for love and a clingy cropped shirt that showed off her trim waist and breasts that bounced slightly as she strode down the sidewalk.

She stopped in front of the For Sale sign attached to the front window, then reached behind the iron burglar bars and yanked on the paper until it came loose. She pulled it free and rolled it up, tucked it under her arm, then went back inside.

"Hold it," Tony said. "Changed my mind. I'll talk to her."

"Uh-oh," Priscilla said. "Watch out, Tony's on the prowl."

He gave Pris a disdainful look. "Daralee and I just broke up. You don't honestly think I'm ready to get involved with someone else, do you?"

Tony's fellow firefighters laughed so hard at this that Otis nearly fell onto the concrete floor and Ethan had to support himself against the truck.

"What? I can't believe you're laughing about my messed-up love life."

"Messed up," Ethan agreed, "until the next girl comes along. You've been mooning about Daralee for, what, a week?"

"We had a good thing going," Tony said more to himself than Ethan. "I really thought…" He stopped.

No time for regrets. That woman with the gold hair was undoubtedly the new owner of Brady's, and someone needed to talk to her before she changed anything. "Cover for me if Captain Campeon notices I'm gone." Without any further hesitation, Tony loped out of the station, darting between cars on busy Jefferson Street, toward the gorgeous goddess of a woman who—unknowingly—waited inside Brady's to meet him.

Brady's Tavern occupied a two-story building that must have been close to a hundred years old, and the brick looked as if it hadn't been cleaned since coal stoves went out of vogue. A flock of pigeons had taken up residence under the eaves and the evidence of their frequent presence covered the cracked sidewalk.

The bar's door wasn't locked, so Tony pushed it open. A wall of hot, stuffy air, heavy with the scent of stale beer, slapped him in the face. "Hello? Anyone home?"

A teenage girl bounded up to him like an eager puppy. "Hi. Who're you?"

"Tony. I work at the fire station across the street. Are you the new owner of Brady's?"

She nodded. "Well, my mom is. This place is so cool. Do you play shuffleboard?"

"Not only do I play, I was the Brady's Tavern shuffleboard champion two years running. Where's your mom?" Surely the woman he'd seen removing the For Sale sign wasn't this girl's mother.

"My mom is Brady's sister. Was. Whatever."

"Then Brady was your uncle. It must have been tough losing him so unexpectedly. He was a great guy."

"Not according to Mom. She said he was a drunkard black sheep who couldn't be trusted with a dime." The girl rocked back on her heels, apparently not realizing she'd insulted someone Tony had considered a friend. And her mother's information was outdated. Brady had quit drinking twenty years ago.

"Could I speak to your mom?" He looked around the bar, which seemed strangely empty without the usual smattering of cops, firefighters and "siren sisters"—the female groupies who were turned on by any man who wore a badge or wielded a hose. But he didn't see the blond woman.

"My mom is at work. But if it's anything to do with Brady's, you'll want to talk to Julie."

"Julie?"

"My sister."

Ah. That made a whole lot more sense.

"She's counting the glasses or something. Trying to decide what to keep and what to get rid of."

Then he'd better talk to her right away before she did something stupid—like throw away the Daryl Jones memorial ashtray.

Tony heard some clinking going on behind the long carved-wood bar and figured that had to be where Julie had disappeared to. He made his way to the bar, his feet *schlup-schlupp*ing with every step on the sticky floor.

Ah, it was good to be back here. Brady's was lit

up like a Christmas tree, with its vintage signs. They covered almost every available bit of wall surface and illuminated the interior, which was crammed full of tables and chairs, pool tables, dartboards—guy heaven. Every corner had a TV, and when the place had been open all of them were always tuned in to a smorgasbord of sporting events.

A lonely silk ficus tree lurked forlornly in a corner, covered with dust. Supposedly one of Brady's girlfriends had put it there one time, trying in vain to class the place up.

"Excuse me, Julie?"

She popped up from behind the bar, a pair of yellow rubber gloves on her hands. Looking startled, she stared at Tony for several seconds of charged silence. She had the most amazing amber eyes. He'd never seen eyes that color before. She reminded him of a golden fawn or an unspoiled woodland nymph.

"Yes?" she finally said. Her low, sexy voice sent shivers down his spine and a rush of blood through his veins.

Tony shook himself out of his daze. How could he be attracted to this woman when his pain over losing Daralee was still so fresh? It was just hormones playing a nasty trick on him. "Hi, I'm Tony Veracruz. I work at the fire station across the street, and we were just wondering…are you going to keep Brady's? We saw that you removed the For Sale sign."

She cocked her head to one side. "Do you want to buy it?"

"Believe me, we've talked about it. But the price tag is a bit high for us working stiffs. We just really miss the place—and Brady. He was a great guy. It was terrible losing him so suddenly. You're his niece?"

"That's right. Julie Polk." She extended her hand across the bar's polished surface, realized she still had gloves on, removed the right one hurriedly and tried again.

Tony took her hand, and rather than shake it as he would a man's, he squeezed it. It was a lovely little hand, with perfectly manicured nails polished a pearly pink. Tony's stomach gave a peculiar swoop.

Julie's mask of detached politeness slipped and a flicker of awareness passed over her face. So she felt it, too?

The teenage girl, who'd come to lean against the bar resting her chin on her folded arms, cleared her throat.

Julie extracted her hand from Tony's. "This is my sister, Belinda. I heard her talking to someone, so I assume you've already met."

"I did have the pleasure, though she didn't volunteer her name. It's a beautiful name, too." He'd almost named his daughter Belinda, so he wasn't deliberately laying it on thick.

Belinda blushed furiously. Though her hair and eyes were darker, she looked much like her sister—which meant she was probably already breaking hearts in all directions.

"So your mother is the new owner of Brady's?" Tony asked Julie.

"Yes. She and Brady owned it together, but she's been more of a silent partner. They weren't very close."

"That's too bad. It's sad when families drift apart." He was thinking about his own family. Due to his parents' multiple marriages, Tony had lots of stepsiblings and half siblings, some of whom he'd lost touch with. "So your mother has decided not to sell?"

"Frankly Mom really doesn't care. She's asked me to deal with it for her." Julie put the second rubber glove back on and resumed her task, which appeared to be counting beer mugs and entering the tally on a clipboard. She gave him a nice view of her denim-clad bottom in the process, which Tony fully enjoyed—until he realized Belinda was smirking at him. He diverted his gaze to the picture of the naked lady above the bar.

"But you are going to reopen?" Tony persisted.

"It would be a shame for the business to leave the family after we've owned it for three generations."

That sounded promising. "Yeah, there's a lot of history here. Who are you gonna get to run the place? Brady had a guy working for him, Alonzo. He'd be a great manager."

"You don't think I could run Brady's?" she asked, challenging. She put the clipboard down and devoted her full attention to their conversation.

"Well, you're..." Tony stopped himself before he

misstepped. Some women had accused him before of being a male chauvinist pig. But it wasn't because he didn't think women deserved equal rights or that they weren't as smart and capable as men. The opposite was more like it. He thought women should be treated better than men. And he didn't think any woman as beautiful and refined as Julie Polk should have to sling beer and deal with groping, drunk customers.

"I'm what?"

"Too pretty to work at a joint like this."

Her gaze fell, her long lashes casting shadows on her smooth cheeks. "Thanks, but I don't have the resources to hire someone else to run the place. And since I'm currently between assignments, as they say, I'm the logical one to take on the job."

"More power to you, then." Tony grinned. Brady's was coming back! The guys at the station would be over the moon. "And don't worry," he added, "you've got lots of friends in the neighborhood who'll help you out. So when are you planning to reopen?"

"Oh, I'd say it'll take a few weeks to refurbish the place, work out the menus…."

"Menus?" Brady had served microwave nachos, popcorn and beer nuts. You didn't need a menu for the basics. "You're going to change Brady's?"

"Brady's is not going to be Brady's." And a big smile spread across her face, dispelling the polite, almost icy mask she'd been wearing and transforming her into an angel. Tony was so entranced with how she looked he almost missed what she said next. "It's going to be Belinda's."

"Belinda's…Bar?" he asked warily.

"Belinda's is going to be the coolest tearoom in all of Dallas."

Julie gathered that sexy Tony Veracruz was not happy with her announcement. He stared, his jaw hanging open, for several seconds as he processed her news.

Lord, he was gorgeous. Those well-defined cheekbones, that smooth olive skin and brown eyes a girl could drown in. Funny, she'd always thought her ex-fiancé, with his aristocratic clean-cut blond handsomeness, was the best-looking guy around. But Tony's earthier looks struck a chord deep inside her.

When he'd said she was pretty, the compliment had given her heart palpitations. But how silly was that? He probably told a half-dozen women a day they were pretty.

"Did you say…?" Tony's voice trailed off.

"Yes, isn't it great? I'm turning Brady's into a tearoom."

"On Jefferson Street?"

"The perfect place, don't you think? Oak Cliff is in the middle of a renaissance. I see revitalization all around us. The historic district is right across the street. Those mansions in Kessler Park are only a mile away. Then there's the Bishop Arts district— lots of sophisticated restaurants and bars going in there." She was using all the same arguments she had used to convince her parents to okay this venture, though truthfully they hadn't cared much what she did with Brady's so long as it brought in some cash.

The moment she'd seen the place, despite its coat of grime, the thought had flashed into her mind: Julie Polk, owner and manager of the classiest tearoom in town. Wouldn't Trey be surprised? When she'd given him back his ring, he'd told her she would never make anything of herself without his help. But she was going to show him and his whole family how wrong they were.

Besides, she also wanted to transform Brady's into Belinda's for herself. After her disastrous broken engagement, she needed something she could call her own; something no one could take away from her.

She resumed counting beer mugs. They were nice, heavy glass ones, and she could use them as iced-tea glasses. Almost everything else would have to go, though. She'd been doing a quick-and-dirty inventory since she and Belinda had arrived this morning, and the results were depressing.

"But Brady's is a neighborhood institution," Tony argued. "You can't close it for good."

"I don't really have a choice," she said practically. "I know absolutely nothing about running a bar. I do, however, know a great deal about managing a tearoom." She'd spent a year as manager of Lochinvar's, the oh-so-tony tearoom inside Bailey-

Davidson's, the upscale department store owned by her ex-fiancé's family.

Belinda's was going to be much cooler than Lochinvar's, which had been around for fifty years and attracted mostly older matrons. Belinda's was going to bring in the younger women, the rich hipsters who frequented Hattie's and Caribe in Bishop Arts—the ones who knew Oak Cliff was the cool place to be, the ones who thought Deep Ellum was just a bit too grungy and Highland Park too stuffy.

"But Brady's is a gold mine," Tony argued, following her along his side of the bar as she moved to count the next shelf of glasses. "It's packed most nights with hard-drinking men and women who buy lots of beer."

"What a charming picture. Anyway, I've looked at the books. The place might have been crowded, but the customers weren't spending enough money. Brady's profits were way down. There's almost no money in the accounts either."

That didn't surprise Tony. "Brady spent it as fast as he could make it. He was a soft touch. He gave money away to any hard-luck story that came his way. He even hosted free Thanksgiving dinners for the homeless."

"He did?" Julie was surprised. According to her mother, Brady had never done anything that didn't directly benefit Brady. "That sounds so nice."

"You didn't know him?"

"Not really. Anyway, the point is, the books don't lie." She'd been taking classes at community college with an eye toward a degree in business management. She knew a bit about accounting. "Brady's was barely breaking even."

"Okay, so maybe the place isn't a gold mine. Yet. But with the right management skills…" He looked pointedly at Julie.

"I've done the research. The demographics are changing. A more upscale establishment on this street will be cutting-edge. Belinda's should be extremely profitable, even with the investments I'll have to make to refurbish the place." Julie was counting on some quick profits. Clever Belinda, with her perfect SAT scores, was going to attend an Ivy League university. And since the Davidsons had withdrawn their pledge to finance Belinda's education, it was up to Julie to figure out how to pay the staggering tuition by next fall, only a year away.

Even though Belinda was certain to get some sort of scholarship, there would still be huge expenses. And her parents couldn't contribute anything. They could barely take care of their own bills.

The real-estate agent had told Julie it could take months or even years to sell Brady's for a fair price. And all the mortgages and liens Brady had on the building would eat up the proceeds from any purchase.

Opening the tearoom was a much better idea. She could sell everything—and there were some collectibles tucked in and around Brady's, like the cigar-store Indian and the vintage pinball machines and neon signs. With the proceeds and her own little nest egg, she could transform this place into a posh yet cozy oasis that would provide her and her family with income for years to come.

Eventually, she would have to pay off Brady's creditors. Fortunately, however, they'd been willing to work out terms when she'd explained she wanted to get the place back in business.

Julie had done the math. She really could manage this.

"You can't do this," Tony said. "Please, Julie, I'm begging you. You'll be destroying a piece of Oak Cliff history."

Julie stopped counting beer mugs. She kept losing track, and who could blame her when this gorgeous man was distracting her? She wondered exactly what he'd be willing to do to get her to change her mind, then immediately banished the thought. She'd broken her engagement less than a month ago. She was still reeling over her fiancé's betrayal and the astounding realization that he and his whole family had expected her to brush his in-discretion under the rug. She had no business letting sexy Tony Veracruz heat up her blood.

"Mr. Veracruz, look around you."

He did. "Yeah?"

"This place is a dump. It's a dive, a blight on a neighborhood that's trying to come back. I'm going to improve it, beautify it, make it a showplace Oak Cliff can be proud of."

"Well, I'll admit Brady's could use a good scrubbing."

"What it could use is a nuclear explosion. That's what it would take to get the dirt off these floors. Everything reeks of stale beer and cigarette smoke."

"You could clean the place up," Tony tried again. "We'd help you."

"I'm sorry, Tony." And truly she was. Brady's had probably been the sort of place where some people felt they belonged. Like Cheers, only grittier. Finding a place to fit in, to belong, was important, and she should know. She'd been trying to figure out where she fit her whole life.

Not in Pleasant Grove, the blue-collar suburb where she'd grown up in a housing project. She'd always known there was something better for her out in the world and she'd thought she'd found her place working at Bailey-Davidson's. She'd devoted nine years of her life to it—watching, studying, improving herself, moving up the department-store career ladder, slowly accumulating college credits so that she would eventually qualify for higher management positions.

She loved that store. She loved being around the beautiful clothes, the delicate bone china, the designer bed linens—oh, how she loved the linens department.

Most of all, she'd loved being around all those well-educated, refined, soft-spoken people. And when Trey Davidson had noticed her, accepted her, when his friends had welcomed her into their circle—even though she couldn't claim an Ivy League affiliation or a single drop of blue blood—she'd thought she'd found her place. Up-and-coming Bailey-Davidson's executive and wife to the store's heir apparent.

A dream come true.

Except the dream had turned into the proverbial nightmare, and Julie had once again found herself afloat in a strange sea in which she didn't belong, wondering what she would do with her life.

Belinda's could be *her* place. Her creation, her universe. She could surround herself with beautiful things, fine foods and people who appreciated the same things she did.

Tony Veracruz, she guessed, would not be one of those people. Which was a pity. Let Marcel at the Bailey-Davidson's salon cut Tony's hair, then put him in an Armani suit, and he'd fit right in at any office in any glass high-rise in the city. But Julie suspected that sort of life didn't appeal to him. She could tell he liked himself the way he was and liked where he was in life.

Which was fine. That was part of his appeal, actually—the fact that he was obviously so comfortable in his skin.

His gorgeous skin.

"How 'bout I take you out to dinner tomorrow?" Tony asked. "We could get some burgers. You could tell me more about this tearoom idea of yours."

Oh, she was tempted. For one thing, she hadn't been out to eat at a real restaurant in weeks because she'd been hoarding her pennies.

But she had an idea that if she let Tony take her out, even for an innocent hamburger, before long he would be telling her more about what a great place Brady's was and how wrong she was to change it to a tearoom, and she would start to doubt herself.

She didn't need that. She'd doubted her judgment enough after finding out the man she loved had been lying to her for months—maybe longer. She needed to surround herself with people who would encourage her and support her and help her make Belinda's a resounding success.

Julie wouldn't have cared so much about this venture if it was just about herself, but she would do whatever it took for Belinda. Her sweet, brilliant baby sister was going to have the chance to make something fantastic of herself, and nothing was going to prevent it. Not the miserable, self-serving Davidsons, not her parents' apathy and certainly not a fireman who was sentimental about a run-down eyesore of a neighborhood bar. Even if he was sexy as hell.

"I'm sorry, Tony. I appreciate the invitation, but I have so much to do," she said coolly. Which was true enough.

"Another time, then. I better get back to work." He flashed her a dazzling grin, turned with a jaunty wave and exited out the squeaky front door.

She hoped he wasn't serious about asking her out again. She might not have the strength to turn down his next invitation.

Chapter Two

"I never met Uncle Brady, did I?" Belinda asked as she and Julie climbed the stairs to the apartment above the bar where Brady had lived.

"No, I don't think you ever met him." She only had a vague memory herself of a big bear of a man who showed up at Thanksgiving with a fruitcake, drank too much wine and was asked to leave. "He sent Mom a little check every once in a while—her part of the 'profits' from the bar. But he and Mom hardly ever talked. Mom sent him a Christmas card every year, but he never reciprocated."

"Tony said he was a great guy."

"Brady probably gave Tony free beer." But Tony had painted an image of Brady that Julie couldn't get out of her mind. A soft touch. Generous and kind. Sure didn't sound like the mooch her mother had described.

"How much do you think we'll get for all that stuff downstairs?" Belinda asked.

"I'll have to do some research, but I bet those vintage signs will fetch a good price."

"What about those green glass lampshades? Trey has some of those, doesn't he?"

Julie gave an unladylike snort. "Trey's are reproductions. Ours are the real thing. In fact, maybe I'll keep those. They'll look pretty in the tearoom, don't you think?"

Belinda shrugged. "Will you keep the jukebox?"

"No, that I'm going to sell. It's an old Wurlitzer, and the vinyl records alone are worth a fortune."

Rather than sounding excited about the prospect, Belinda gave a sad little huff.

"What?"

"Oh, it's just a bit tragic thinking about tearing the place up."

"Belinda, you must be joking. It's disgusting."

"Yeah, but that guy Tony was right. If you scrubbed it up, it wouldn't be so bad."

"Don't even think about it. I'm not running a bar." Even if she had the experience or knowledge, she preferred the idea of improving the neighborhood. Brady's had been an eyesore, no doubt drawing unsavory characters. Belinda's was going to be beautiful. Maybe the firefighters were unhappy about her planned changes, but she bet most of the residents around here would be delighted.

"I know, I know," Belinda said. "I'm just saying it's a little sad, that's all."

Julie tried several keys from the big key ring the lawyer had given her mother, finally locating the right one. She'd been avoiding the place where her uncle had died, but she knew she had to check it out. She was planning to live here while she oversaw the renovations—and maybe afterward, too. It would save her a long commute to work, plus she would have her privacy back. Living in her parents' tiny house, where they were all on top of each other and getting on each other's nerves, wasn't going to work for much longer.

This apartment would do until she could afford something better. Someday, she'd like to have her own house. It didn't have to be anything as grand as Trey's Highland Park house, where she would be living now if she hadn't canceled the wedding. But she wanted a front porch. And flower boxes in the windows. And a real backyard, maybe with a deck where she could sit outside on a Sunday morning and read the paper, a golden retriever by her side.

Still, a one-bedroom apartment rent-free wasn't bad. She held her breath and pushed open the door.

Brady's living space was surprisingly neat, clean and spartan, given the excessive grime and clutter of the bar. Julie had always heard Brady described as a man who couldn't be trusted. *Lazy, slovenly, a freeloader*—those were words her mother commonly used to describe Brady. Yet that image didn't match his digs.

Julie poked around to see if there might be any valuables, but aside from a couple of old paintings and some vintage Fiesta dishes, nothing jumped out as a real treasure.

The bedroom was empty except for a dresser. Someone had removed the bed in which Brady had expired, which was a huge relief. No way would Julie have been able to sleep there.

She returned to the living room and sank onto a worn sofa. It was pretty soft—she could sleep on this. And Belinda would be happy to get her own room back at their parents' house. The sisters had been sharing a room and a bed, just like old times, for the past couple of weeks.

"So what do you think?" Belinda asked. "Can you live here?"

"Sure. I've lived in worse places." Her first apartment—when she'd gotten her first real job as a stock girl at Bailey-Davidson's—had been one ratty room in the attic of an old East Dallas house. She'd done her cooking on a hot plate.

Brady's living quarters were a palace compared to that but something of a comedown from her last place—a classy Park Cities town house she'd rented from the Davidsons. Still, she had a little money to live on, the proceeds from returning all the wedding presents—the ones her friends and family had refused to take back. And Trey's parents had given her a handsome "severance check" in return for her silence about his little secret, which she'd been happy to accept—not that she ever would have gone blabbing about the illegitimate child he'd conceived with his mistress even as he'd been planning a lavish wedding to Julie. Gossip like that would only make *her* look dumb. Her stash was enough to keep her going until the tearoom opened.

"The view is certainly nice," Belinda said dreamily.

Julie glanced out the window to see what her sister was talking about. All she could see was the fire station, a hundred-year-old brick monstrosity in need of a good sandblasting.

Then she looked closer and realized the blinds to the second-floor window were open; inside a man was pulling off his T-shirt. "Belinda!"

"What? I can look, can't I?"

Julie joined her sister at the window. The man picked up a barbell and started doing some curls. It was none other than her firefighting Adonis. "He's doing that on purpose."

"Oh, like he knew we'd be up here, staring out the window? Get a grip, Jules. You're paranoid."

Maybe she was. But her reaction to Tony Veracruz had unnerved her.

She'd once felt that way about Trey. He'd flirted with her shamelessly, focused all his attention on her, swept her off her feet. She'd fallen in love, hard, with a man she thought she knew. Handsome, smart, ambitious, funny, generous…

Unfaithful.

Feeling all gooey inside over a man, getting caught up in flirtation and charm—none of those offered any guarantee of that man's deep-down character. Julie would do well to remember that and to focus on building a secure future for herself without relying on anyone else.

Tony looked out the window, saw them staring and flashed that cocky smile.

Julie abruptly closed the blinds.

"Hey!" Belinda objected.

"He's too old for you."

"But not for you. Earlier, he was checking out your butt."

"Really?" Despite herself, Julie felt a little thrill. "He probably checks out every girl's butt."

"He didn't look at mine. Besides, he's going to be your neighbor. You have to be friendly."

"No, I don't." Tony Veracruz was trouble with a capital *T*, and she certainly didn't need any more of that.

"So ARE YOU GOING TO tell us what happened?" Priscilla asked. As busy as their shift had been earlier, activity had died down completely. Pris was killing time in Station 59's exercise room, running on the treadmill.

Priscilla was a maniac when it came to fitness and she'd guilted almost every firefighter on their shift into working out more. It was humiliating when a wisp of a woman like Pris could lift more weight than you.

Tony had found it difficult to admit to his co-workers the horrible news about what was happening to Brady's Tavern. They'd given him a task: convince the bar's new owner to reopen Brady's just as it was. And though he knew he had nothing to do with Julie's decision to turn Brady's into a tea-room, he still felt as if he'd let down his comrades.

Mission failed.

Not only that, but beautiful Julie Polk had said no when he'd asked her out. Oh, she was interested. She'd acted a little fluttery when he'd told her she was pretty, and he'd felt some definite vibes flash through the air between them. But she'd been prickly, too. Her mind was so filled with plans for her tearoom that romance was way down on her priority list.

He knew darn well he shouldn't be thinking about romance either. He was still smarting from Daralee's sudden rejection. He'd thought their rela-tionship was going somewhere. They'd been so crazy about each other. Now he knew he'd been nothing but a boy toy to her, someone to irk her exhusband. When that hadn't worked, he'd become history.

But just looking at Julie sent his hormones into a frenzy. Could he help it if he liked having a girl-friend? Still, the next time he fell head over heels for someone, he wanted the same feelings in return. He didn't want to be a low priority or an after-thought.

"Earth to Tony," Priscilla said impatiently. "Did you hear me?"

Sooner or later everyone would find out about Julie's plans. He might as well break the news. "I heard you. It's just too horrible what she's doing to Brady's."

Priscilla gasped. "Is she tearing down the building? Granted, it needs work, but isn't it a historical landmark or something?"

"She's doing worse than that. It's sacrilege."

Now he had Ethan's and Otis's attention, too. And Jim Peterson's. "Would you just tell us instead of being a drama queen?" said Peterson, pedaling at a leisurely pace on the stationary bike.

"She's turning Brady's into a tearoom."

Otis dropped his barbell with a clang. Ethan's jaw sagged.

Priscilla, however, didn't appear horrified. "A tearoom. Right here in our neighborhood."

Ethan groaned. "Only you, Priscilla, would find this news welcome."

"I would miss Brady's, but a tearoom could be good. I could do lunch there."

Otis threw his sweaty towel at her. "And where exactly are us men supposed to hang out?"

Priscilla turned off the treadmill and slowed to a stop. "At least maybe we could get some healthy food there. A salad or…" Loud groans cut her off. She shrugged. "I can't help you if you won't help yourselves."

"Pris, maybe *you* should talk to her," Tony said. "Woman to woman. Tell her how important Brady's is to this neighborhood. It's important for us and the cops to have a neutral place to meet and talk things over."

Pris gave Tony an appraising look. "If you can't convince her, I don't have a chance. Is she married?"

"I don't think so." He hadn't seen a ring, anyway.

"You're just gonna have to try harder," Ethan said.

"Seduce her," Otis added. "Once she's sleeping with you, she'll have to listen to you. Chicks are like that."

Priscilla threw the sweaty towel back at Otis. "Typical male logic. *Men* think with their gonads. Women think with their brains."

"Just give it the old college try," Ethan said. "Get to know her, let her get to know you and then convince her to reopen Brady's. We're sick of seeing you mope about Daralee. About time you found a new girlfriend."

Tony couldn't deny he wanted to give Julie another try—smart move or not. Since meeting her a few minutes earlier, he'd had a hard time remembering exactly why he'd thought he was in love with Daralee. But cold-blooded seduction wasn't his game. He liked women. He didn't like the idea of using them, even for a good cause. And then there was his own much-stomped-on heart to think of.

"I'd love to have a new girlfriend," Tony said more candidly than he'd meant to. He focused on Ethan. "I want what you and Kat have. But I'm not sure Julie's the one to provide it. She's a tough cookie."

Ethan shook his head as he wiped down the weight bench he'd been using. "If you go in with that attitude, *expecting* to strike out…"

"Look," said Otis, "here's what you do. You harden your heart. Every time you look at Julie, you think Daralee. You remember how bad she treated you. You remind yourself that women are evil incarnate."

"Hey," Priscilla objected.

"Present company excluded," Otis said quickly. He'd been one of the ones to object the loudest when the fire station got invaded by a woman, but he and Priscilla had formed an unlikely friendship, surprising everyone. "If you feel yourself softening even a little bit toward this Julie person, you come talk to me and I'll set you straight."

Tony supposed Otis would be the one to do that. He had three ex-wives. "If you're such an expert, why don't you seduce her?"

"Me?" He gave a loud, hearty laugh and patted his gut. "That girl isn't looking for a fat, old black man. She's looking for a young stud like you. Besides, my Ruby would kill me if I went near that sweet young thing."

The P.A. system crackled to life. "Dinner is now being served in the kitchen," Lt. Murph McCrae's gruff voice announced. "Come get it now or go hungry."

The firefighters didn't have to be asked twice. They tromped down the stairs in a hungry stampede. But before they could sit down, the alarm sounded. And before they'd even climbed into their turnout gear, a second alarm went out.

"Sounds big," Tony said, pushing thoughts of Julie out of his mind for the moment. Another dose of adrenaline surged through his body. He was on the ladder truck today with Ethan, the captain and Jim Peterson. He hadn't been to many big fires, and just the thought of descending on a big conflagration got him as excited as a young kid at an amusement park.

This one was big, too. It was at a run-down autobody shop, which meant gasoline, oil—potential explosions.

"IC to Ladder 59," came the incident commander's voice over the radio. "Need y'all on the B side of the building on ventilation. Start getting those walls down, if you can."

Captain Campeon, on the ladder truck, abruptly ordered a change of direction, and the truck turned down a side street, raced through an alley and parked in a vacant lot just behind the burning building. Tony chugged the remainder of a bottle of water. On a hot day like today, it paid to stay hydrated.

"Grab your tools, rookies," Campeon ordered. Tony did as he was told, collecting an ax and a pike pole. Then he took up a position at veteran Jim Peterson's elbow. That was his only assignment— stick to Peterson like bubblegum. The hot August sun would roast him alive inside his turnout gear if he stood out in it for long.

"Basque," Campeon barked, "get a ladder up to that roof. Peterson, Veracruz, get the window."

The window was barred, but it was easy enough to break the glass using their pikes. As soon as they did, smoke poured out and that was when they heard a dog howling inside.

Tony hated the thought of a helpless animal dying in a fire. Normally, firefighters would rescue pets if it was possible to do so without dramatically endangering themselves.

"Hell, let's see if we can get to him," Peterson said. The back door was solid-core steel, but the walls were thin corrugated tin. Tony whacked at the wall with his ax and then Peterson yanked at it until they had an opening.

"Ladder 59 to IC, there's a dog inside. Request permission to enter and try to get him out. Not much fire back here."

"Affirmative, Ladder 59."

"I'll go first," Peterson said to Tony, pulling on his air mask as he set one leg through the jagged opening.

With his own breathing mask in place, Tony climbed in right after Peterson.

They'd no sooner gotten inside than a blur of brown fur rushed at them. It flew through the air and latched on to Jim Peterson's arm, growling furiously. The dog, a pit bull mix, wasn't huge, but it was determined.

Peterson fell back on his butt, cursing wildly. "Get this damn thing off me!"

Tony gave the dog a kick. And when that didn't dislodge it, he prodded it firmly with the flat side of his ax. He didn't want to kill the creature, but he didn't want it to maim his superior, either.

The dog remained firmly attached.

"Ladder 59 to IC," Tony said into his radio, trying

not to sound panicked. "We need some water back here, fast!"

But the call for help was unnecessary; two men were already approaching with a hose. They saw the situation for what it was and blasted the dog with a hard stream of water.

The spray nearly drowned Peterson, but the dog let go. It leaped through the makeshift door and was gone. Tony had never seen a dog run that fast.

"You okay, Jim?" Tony asked, helping Peterson to his feet.

"No. Damn dog has sharp teeth and the jaws of death."

Just as they were emerging through the opening in the wall, an air horn sounded, the signal to evacuate the building. It was too dangerous to remain. Tony was surprised: the building hadn't looked all that bad inside.

An ambulance had already pulled around to the vacant lot in back as Peterson and Tony emerged. Peterson yanked off his mask, his face tightened in pain. Tony couldn't see any blood—until Peterson took off his coat.

His arm was a mess.

Once the paramedics took over, Tony located Ethan and Captain Campeon. They were as baffled as he was about why they'd been told to clear the building. The fire seemed to be under control.

A few moments later, however, they found out why.

Two incendiary devices had been found at opposite ends of the structure and one on the roof. By now, everyone knew what to look for; this was unmistakably the work of their serial arsonist. Planting a vicious attack dog on the scene was his latest trick to inflict bodily damage on firefighters. Not as showy as the deadly warehouse fire, in which the roof had been rigged to collapse, but still clever and mean. And there was no guarantee he hadn't planted other booby traps inside. At the previous fire he'd set a pipe bomb that fortunately hadn't detonated.

A fire marshal's Suburban showed up as Tony and Ethan cleaned and loaded their tools, talking in hushed voices about the arsonist. Captain Roark Epperson, lead investigator on the case, stepped out, his face grim.

Tony knew Epperson from the training academy; he'd been an instructor there. He also knew Epperson from hanging out at Brady's Tavern. They'd crossed swords over the shuffleboard table a few times.

The ambulance took Peterson to the hospital for stitches and a shot of antibiotics, so Tony took the rare opportunity to sit beside the captain.

"Epperson's gotta be taking this hard," Campeon said as he pulled their truck out of the alley. They drove slowly past the front of the building. Roark was standing in the street, talking to one of the remaining firefighters. "Hey, is that Priscilla he's talking to?"

"Yeah," Tony and Ethan said together. Priscilla had been riding on the engine.

"How does he know her?"

"He was our arson instructor at the academy," Tony answered. "And we've run into him a few times at Brady's."

Campeon snorted. "Brady's. Damn shame. That niece has no idea the disservice she's doing to the community by destroying that bar." He turned to Tony. "Didn't I hear you were doing something about that, Romeo?"

"He's flakin' out on us," Ethan said. "He struck out once, so he's not even gonna try again."

"I didn't say that," Tony argued. In truth, he was still making up his mind.

"You gotta try," Campeon said, showing a rare degree of humanity. Normally he remained stoic and stone-faced no matter was going on around him. "You gotta get through to her. A tearoom? Holy cripes."

All right, Tony would do it—for Brady's. After all, his captain had just given him an order, right? He would seduce Julie Polk. He would pretend he wanted to help her get her tearoom open, but while he was doing it he would share stories about Brady's that would appeal to her sentimentality. He would use every strategy he could think of to get her to change her mind.

Most importantly, he would *not* fall in love with her. He would not set himself up for more heartbreak.

Chapter Three

Julie was afraid this time she'd bitten off more than she could chew. In her zeal to maximize profits from the liquidation of her uncle's estate, she'd decided an auction was the way to go. She'd done her research and estimated the value of most of the collectibles, putting a reserve price on anything really worthwhile so it wouldn't walk out the door for nothing. Then she'd hired an auctioneer, picked a date and paid for an expensive display ad in the newspaper as well as in a local antiques-and-collectibles weekly.

The auction was two days away—and the bar was still a wreck. She'd had every intention of getting in here and cleaning things so that the items would fetch the highest prices. She'd also planned to get a ladder and take down the tin ceiling—each panel was worth at least ten bucks. But she'd ended up staying home to care for her dad for a couple of days instead when the woman who regularly looked in on him developed a cold. Since Julie had been living back at home for several weeks, she'd felt it was the least she could do. Otherwise her mom would have had to miss work.

Now her dad's caregiver was back, but Julie was so far behind she knew she'd never catch up. She had a dozen different cleaning products, a bucket full of old rags and not nearly enough time or elbow grease to do the job. Belinda, working double shifts at her summer waitress job this week, wasn't available.

Well, nothing for Julie to do but jump into the project and get as much done as she could. She'd found an old ladder in a back closet. She could take down at least one of the ceiling panels and shine it up so bidders could get a good look at the intricate pressed pattern.

She climbed the rungs and balanced herself precariously at the top. With a screwdriver and a hammer she tried to pry one of the tiles loose, but they'd been up there for almost a hundred years and they weren't coming down easily.

Finally she managed to get the hammer's claw wedged under one corner. She pried with all her strength but got nowhere.

The front door opened and a shaft of morning sun cut through the bar's dusty interior. Belatedly, Julie realized she should have locked the door behind her. This part of Oak Cliff wasn't a hotbed of violent crime, but a girl couldn't be too careful.

A man stepped inside, silhouetted in the doorway, and for a few moments Julie couldn't see his features. Then she recognized the broad shoulders, that muscular chest, the dominating presence. She took in a deep breath. It was Tony.

Even as she'd teemed with ideas for Belinda's tearoom, making lists and budgets and plans, Tony Veracruz had never been far from her thoughts. And at night when she couldn't sleep—and these days, she never could sleep—he invaded her fantasies.

She'd told herself it was harmless to imagine what he looked like naked, that she would have few if any dealings with him in the future, so long as she kept her blinds drawn. Given her flat refusal to even talk about reopening Brady's or consider accepting his offer of dinner, she hadn't expected him to return, invading her solitude and setting her heart vibrating like a tuning fork.

She started to say something—and then everything happened at once. With an ear-splitting noise, the tin panel above her pulled partly free, revealing a wooden beam seething with termites.

Dozens of them fell into her hair.

She screamed and dropped her hammer, then lost her balance. Clawing at the air as she fell backward, she braced herself to hit the hard wooden floor. She wondered in the split second she was airborne how many bones she would break.

But she didn't hit the floor. Instead, she fell into a strong pair of arms as perfectly and neatly as if she'd fallen into a hammock.

How had he gotten there so quickly? It took her a few moments to realize she was okay; she wasn't going to die after all. "What are you doing here?" she asked inanely.

"Is that any way to greet a man who just saved your life?"

"Put me down, please." She still had a head full of termites. She had to get them off her.

"You could have broken your neck. Why didn't you ask someone to help you with this?"

"Oh, you mean a big, strong man—because I couldn't possibly wield a couple of tools?"

"Well, obviously you…"

"I'm perfectly capable! Or I was, until an entire nest of termites flew into my hair."

"Termites?"

"There are a couple on your arm now."

He quickly put her down and brushed at his arm, while she shook the rest of the insects out of her hair. Ugh. Her skin was still crawling from the sight of those awful bugs.

"Got any Raid?" Tony asked.

"It's going to take more than bug spray, I'm afraid." She mentally added a termite inspection, fumigation and possibly expensive repairs to her working list of things to take care of. For now, though…where had she seen bug spray? The storeroom? She walked back to look.

Tony was right at her heels. "You're taking down the ceiling?"

"I'd planned to auction off the ceiling, along with all this other stuff. But I didn't know there was nothing but bare rafters behind the tin. I guess I'll have to leave it. Ah, here it is. For crawling and flying insects. I think termites are both."

Tony took the can from her. "I'll take care of this." He climbed up the ladder and sent a toxic fog into the space above the ceiling panels. "You know, the tin ceiling is part of the ambience," he argued as dead bugs fell to the floor. "Anyway, this is a historical landmark. You can't go tearing it up."

Julie stood well away from the bug shower. "I checked with the landmark commission. So long as I don't make material changes to the exterior, I'm okay. And a tin ceiling isn't exactly the ambience I'm looking for."

Painted tin ceilings were funky and kind of charming, but Julie was going for classy all the way. She'd wanted to do textured plaster.

She mentally adjusted her picture of Belinda's to reflect a tin ceiling—painted a pale yellow so as not to call attention to itself. It would be okay.

Then she realized something was on her foot— something alive. Immediately thinking *termite,* she started to kick until she realized it was a half-grown Dalmatian puppy gnawing on her shoelace.

"Excuse me," she said, yanking her foot away, "have we met?"

Tony came down from the ladder. "This is Bluto. His mom is Daisy, the fire station mascot. I usually give him a walk on my days off."

"They let you keep puppies at the fire station?"

"Only in a dog run in the back. And only temporarily. The pups had to go. Bluto is the last one."

"So you brought him here?"

"I saw the lights on and thought I'd stop in and see how it's going." He looked around. "You still have a lot of work to do, I see."

"Rub it in, why don't you?" Her attention was torn between gorgeous Tony and his cute puppy, which wagged its tail so hard its entire body wiggled.

She couldn't help it. She bent down to pet the pup, and it jumped all over, licking her face in a frenzy of love. Her parents hadn't allowed any pets, seeing them simply as more mouths to feed. And once she was on her own, she'd never considered getting a dog or cat.

"Hi, Bluto." It was much easier to be warm and friendly to the puppy than to Tony. Safer, too. She wasn't normally *un*friendly, but she knew she had to be on her guard with Tony for two reasons: he wanted something from her she couldn't give, and she wanted something from him she didn't dare ask for. If he had any idea how attracted she was to him, he could use it against her.

"So you live around here?" she asked.

"Just down Willomet. Less than a block."

They were neighbors.

A noise above her yanked her attention away from the pup. She looked up just in time to see the ceiling panel she'd been working on detach itself completely and head straight for her.

Tony grabbed Julie and the dog and yanked them both out of the way. The heavy piece of tin, with its knife-sharp edges, crashed to the floor right where she'd been standing, leaving a gouge in the wooden planking.

Now she reacted. She'd almost died—twice in two minutes. Her knees went wobbly, and if Tony hadn't put his arms around her, she'd have sunk to the floor.

"That's twice I've saved your life," he said, his voice husky.

For an insane moment, Julie thought he might kiss her. She'd fantasized about it often enough over the past couple of days. But then the moment passed, sanity reasserted itself and Tony released her, leaving her tingling.

Could a brush with death cause these peculiar feelings? She sure hoped she had an excuse for wanting to lose herself in a man's touch when she was supposed to be concentrating on her tearoom.

With no small effort, Tony pulled himself out of the sensual fog that Julie had put him in. He'd felt so drawn to her, as if he wanted to kiss her. Thankfully he'd realized how inappropriate that would be and had let the woman go, taking a step back to put her out of temptation's reach. This seduction had to be executed with care.

Ethan had said to make friends with Julie, get to know her. That wasn't Tony's normal approach. He usually liked to sweep a woman off her feet, flirt mercilessly, prove to her how strongly he was attracted to her. He'd always figured the friendship could come later, when the sexual pull wasn't so overwhelming that it occupied all of his brain cells.

But so far that friendship part had eluded him. Yeah, he was friends with Priscilla and Ethan's wife, Kat—and Natalie, the mother of his little girl. As far as his love life went, though, something always went wrong before he could become friends with a lover.

So maybe he would try being friends first. There was more than one way to seduce a woman, and he wouldn't quit until he'd tried them all.

"Th-thank you," Julie said, recovering some of the color in her face. "I do appreciate the life-saving maneuvers."

"That's what firefighters are for." She looked amazing, standing there with her heaving breasts and her rosy cheeks, her golden hair mussed from shaking. She was trying to pretend that being so close to him hadn't had much effect, but Tony knew better.

Then she pulled herself together, all business again. "As you pointed out, I have a ton of work to do. So if you'll excuse me…"

"That's why I'm here. I thought I could help."

She narrowed her eyes suspiciously. "Why would you offer to help when you hate the idea of my tearoom?"

He shrugged. "Never could resist a damsel in distress." He looked around. "And you are in distress."

He could tell she wanted to argue. But her need for an extra pair of hands and some elbow grease won out. "If you really want to help, the wooden Indian would make a good start. He's covered with so much nicotine I can't even tell what color he's supposed to be." Then she added, "But you won't soften me up. I won't change my mind about the tea-room. So if that's your agenda…"

"Agenda? You've got to be kidding," Tony said, his conscience pinching him a bit as he picked up a cleaning rag. At least if he helped her clean, he had an excuse to stick around and get to know her better. And she could get to know him. Once she thought it through, she'd realize what a great guy he was—saving her life, helping her scrub this place down—and she might be more willing to listen to his reasons for wanting to revive Brady's Tavern.

Or he might just make love to her. Right now, that seemed a far more intriguing goal than changing her mind about keeping Brady's intact.

"I'm not sure how Sir Edward will feel about taking a bath," Tony said as he tackled decades of filth.

"Sir Edward?"

"The cigar man. He used to belong to an Englishman who owned a cigar shop down on Jefferson. When that gentleman fell on hard times he closed the shop—and he didn't have enough money to pay off his bar tab. So Brady—that would have been the second Brady, your grandfather—took the Indian as payment."

Tony watched Julie from the corner of his eye. She paused in her efforts to clean years of scum off one of the high round tables that dotted Brady's. "Really? How interesting."

She didn't sound sarcastic, at least. So she enjoyed local history. That had to be a good thing for the campaign to save Brady's.

"Are there more stories like that?"

"Dozens." Tony gave up on the Indian and walked back to the bar. "Where's the ashtray that was sitting here?"

"The big ugly one that possibly used to be brass?"

"Yeah."

"I didn't figure anyone would want it, so I threw it away."

Tony clutched at his chest and pretended to gasp for air. "Threw it away?"

"Was it special?" She actually sounded concerned.

"It was the Daryl Jones memorial ashtray. Jones was a legendary fire chief, back in the days of prohibition. When he died, they took the old fire bell down and made an ashtray out of it. He and Brady—that would be your great-grandfather— were good friends."

Julie winced. "And they made his bell into an *ashtray?* Isn't that kind of disrespectful?"

"Since Jones was a chain-smoker, no. I can't believe you threw it away. I'd have bought it from you. Any of the firefighters would have."

Without a word, Julie disappeared into the back room. He heard her digging around and a minute or so later she emerged triumphantly with the ashtray in hand. "If you'll help me clean, you can have the ashtray for free."

"Deal."

As they worked, Tony told her more stories. The

billiard table had come from Dallas's first bowling alley just before it was torn down. The dartboard had been a gift from a baseball player in the 1950s.

Tony showed Julie a bullet hole in the wall that was reputed to have been put there by the famous bank robber Clyde Barrow, of Bonnie and Clyde fame, when Brady's had been a speakeasy.

Julie paused often to take notes.

"That popcorn machine behind the bar came from the Texas Theater down the street."

"No kidding? Hey, they've renovated that theater, haven't they?"

"Yeah, and it looks great." Now he was getting somewhere. "Oak Cliff is renovating everything. People are really starting to appreciate the history of this area. Preserving rather than tearing down." *Hint, hint, Julie.*

"That's marvelous! I bet the theater owners would love to buy back this machine and display it there."

Tony sighed. "What are you writing all these stories down for?"

"The auctioneer says that anything with historical significance will get a better price. So tell me more."

Tony realized his efforts to convince Julie not to tear up Brady's might actually be counterproductive. His stories made her even more inclined to parcel out all these wonderful old things.

Watching her as she scrubbed the filth off an old hurricane lamp—probably something left over from the days before the bar had electricity—he had a hard time remembering what his mission was. He just wanted to kiss her.

Still, he made one more try. "I understand your wanting to get money for all this stuff," he said carefully. "But doesn't sentimental value count for anything? Separately, you have some semivaluable collectibles. Together, you have a legend—your family's legend at that. This is the place your great-grandfather opened a century ago. Doesn't that mean anything to you?"

She looked stung by his harsh question, at first, and then she looked mad—and he knew he'd gone too far. She threw down her rag and marched over to him, getting right in his face.

"I'm sorry that you guys have lost your hangout. Truly I am. But I have to do what's right for me and my family. My living family, not a bunch of dead guys. And even if you try to deny it, it'll be good for the neighborhood, too."

He started to say something, but she cut him off.

"I am not going to change my mind. What do I have to do to convince you?"

Bluto chose that moment to jump against Tony's leg and yip.

"Maybe you should take him for that walk," Julie suggested, her voice softening.

"Yeah, I'll take him back to his mom. He's looking for a good home, by the way."

"That's all I need—a dog to make my life complete. Why don't you keep him?"

Tony laughed. "I already adopted one." He hooked Bluto's leash to his collar and the dog proceeded to drag him toward the door. "Goodbye, Julie. But I'll be back."

As he stepped out into the August heat, he acknowledged that this battle was going to be a lot harder than he'd first thought. But Julie wasn't immune to him. She'd enjoyed the stories he told. Maybe, after she had time to think about it, she would change her mind. And if not…

He could at least get the word out about the auction. Every off-duty cop and firefighter in Oak Cliff would want to attend and grab a piece of Brady's.

As Tony crossed the street, intending to return Bluto to his dog run behind Station 59, he realized he'd forgotten to take the Daryl Jones memorial ashtray.

JULIE HAD BEEN HOPING for a good crowd at the auction, but the mass of people crowding up to the bar to register and receive their bidding numbers exceeded all her expectations.

She'd done everything she could think of to publicize the auction, including the well-placed ads. She'd asked her auctioneer if she should have the sale at an auction house, but he'd discouraged her from that. The bar itself was plenty big enough. The location was easy to find and she would save the costs of renting a hall and transporting the goods. Plus, she would get some locals who would bid on items for sentimental reasons.

The crowd was made up mostly of men in jeans and T-shirts. They didn't look like collectors or antiques dealers. But, then again, how would she know what such people looked like?

The one man she'd been most anxious to see wasn't in the crowd, however. Tony had left abruptly two days earlier, without his darned old ashtray. She felt bad about the way they'd parted, with her all mad. She shouldn't have let him get to her. If she were one hundred percent confident in her plans, his arguments should have just harmlessly rolled off her back. But the truth was, she was scared to death of what she was attempting.

Maybe she'd managed a tearoom, but she'd never started her own business from the ground up. She was a mass of insecurities.

The quality of her sleep had deteriorated still more, because she couldn't get the feel of Tony's embrace out of her mind—nor the way he'd looked into her eyes just before releasing her.

But she had to. Getting involved with a sexy firefighter—or any man, for that matter—wasn't in her plans.

An older man in a suit approached her and she pointed to the clipboard sitting on the bar. "Fill out your name, address and phone there and I'll assign you a number."

"I'm not here to buy, Ms. Polk."

She looked up sharply, alarmed by his stern tone. "Then what can I help you with?"

He held up a badge for her to see. "I'm the fire

marshal. There's a strict limit of one hundred people for these premises, in terms of fire safety, and you've already exceeded that limit."

"A hundred?" Surely that was wrong. The number seemed very low to her. Her building wasn't huge, but it wasn't a broom closet, either. "Are you sure?"

"It's posted by the door. This old building is a historic landmark, which means we take extra care. Have you had the sprinkler system inspected?"

"I'll be doing a complete renovation, and fire safety will be my number one priority," she assured him. "But for the auction, I can't just go kicking people out who've already registered."

"I'm afraid you'll have to, ma'am. Unless you want me to do it. But then I'd have to charge you a hefty fine."

Julie was steaming. The firefighters were behind this, she was sure of it. They'd probably been searching for some way to foil her auction—and they'd found it. Maybe the maximum occupancy was a hundred, but she doubted it had ever been enforced until now.

She supposed she had no choice but to comply with the fire marshal's order. The auction was starting in fifteen minutes.

So she went to the auctioneer's microphone, turned it on and announced that all those who hadn't registered, plus those with numbers higher than ninety-seven, would have to leave because of the fire code. Including herself, Belinda and the auctioneer, that made one hundred. Her announcement produced lots of grumbling, but everyone complied. Once the extras had left, there was plenty of room in the bar. She smelled a rat, especially when the fire marshal shot her a victorious smile.

He parked himself at the door, keeping careful count of all those who came in and those who left.

As the auction progressed, Julie was increasingly disappointed in the results. She'd been to a few similar events before, and usually there was heated bidding, at least over some of the items. But with her auction, once someone bid, the rest of the crowd stayed maddeningly silent. She'd put modest reserve prices on the more valuable things, and most of these did not achieve the minimum bid and so remained unsold.

The auctioneer was sweating, talking up individual items, sharing the stories Julie had written down for him. Finally, though, he shrugged his shoulders and shot her a bewildered glance, validating her own feelings that this was an aberration.

Was it fixed? She took a closer look at the predominantly male, casually dressed crowd, and an awful realization occurred.

They were firefighters. Cops and firefighters. Every single blasted one of them. And they were cooperating, to ensure she did not succeed.

Her face grew hot. How could they be so hateful? Such bad sports? Couldn't they accept that Brady's was gone now and leave her alone? How could anyone get so riled up over a stupid old bar, even if it was a historic landmark?

She caught the eye of one man who'd bid on the wooden Indian and gotten it for a hundred dollars when she knew it was worth a lot more. But she'd purposely set her minimum bids low because she wanted this stuff gone. He gave her a potent, malevolent look, confirming her suspicions.

There wasn't a thing she could do. It was probably illegal for a group of people to get together and refuse to bid against each other, but who was she going to call? The cops? They'd arrived early and gotten in line, ensuring they would fill in all the low-numbered slots, and the fire marshal had done the rest of the work to keep out legitimate collectors and antiques dealers.

The auction was over in less than two hours, and she watched dejectedly as items from Brady's went out the door—the neon lights, the rickety tables and chairs, the dartboards and pool tables, the TVs, even the liquor. A bottle of aged scotch was the one thing that had elicited spirited bidding.

Clem, the auctioneer, approached Julie with a sheepish look. "I'm really sorry, Ms. Polk. I don't know what happened. I gave it my best shot, but these folks just weren't in a bidding mood."

She patted his arm. "It's okay, Clem. I know you did your best. Just bad luck." And some conniving firefighters.

Chapter Four

The fire marshal had gone, and a woman entered the bar, heading straight for Julie. She was about Julie's age and very beautiful, with light brown hair subtly highlighted with gold and a complexion that indicated she took care of her skin.

Her clothes were good quality, too. Lord knew, Julie could spot such things. The woman also looked vaguely familiar. She'd probably shopped in the department store or eaten in the tearoom.

"Are you Julie?" the woman asked.

"Yes, that's me." Julie held out her hand, and the woman shook it in a businesslike fashion.

"Priscilla Garner. I understand a number of your items didn't meet their reserve prices."

Julie mentally snapped her fingers. *Priscilla Garner, of course!* Julie should have recognized her. Her parents were friends of the Davidsons. "Yes, that's right."

"I'll take them off your hands."

"You'll pay the reserve?"

"Well, no. But I'll give you something for them."

Julie figured she couldn't afford to be on her high horse. Maybe she'd set those reserve prices too high. She and Priscilla did some horse trading, and in the end they reached an agreement. Julie would be getting a little more than half what she'd hoped for, but it was better than nothing.

The one thing she hadn't sold was the carved wooden bar, and she was secretly glad about that. No one was willing to pay the steep price she'd put on it, and she wasn't about to take less. Once she'd polished it, it was pretty impressive. She could incorporate it into the design of the tearoom. She'd already decided she would play up the historic-landmark angle. With the money she'd raised—quite a bit less than she'd planned on—she didn't have many options but to make lemonade from the lemons she was stuck with.

The place was almost deserted. Clem had taken off, Belinda had gone to her waitress job and only a few of the bidders remained, working out how to transport and pack some of the larger items they'd bought.

And that was when Tony showed up.

Earlier, she'd been feeling conciliatory toward him, but now that she'd figured out the firefighters' conspiracy, she hardened her heart. He was the enemy.

She pretended not to see him as she cleaned up some glassware that had mysteriously "accidentally" gotten broken. But he apparently wasn't looking for her. He stopped to talk to Priscilla, who'd been heading for the door, intent on finding help in moving the items she'd purchased.

Julie couldn't help but overhear their conversation.

"Hey, Pris. I thought you couldn't get in."

"I couldn't, but I came in after the auction was over. I made a deal for some of the unsold items. I got your shuffleboard table." She headed on out the door.

So Priscilla was in league with the firefighters. If Julie had known that, she'd have told the woman to go soak her head. But, no, that probably wouldn't have been wise. Priscilla and her crowd were exactly the type of people Julie wanted to attract to the tearoom. She'd better be careful.

Tony walked up to Julie, his footsteps bouncing, as if nothing was wrong. "Looks like you had an accident."

"No accident. Someone did it on purpose."

"What happened?" He seemed concerned, but it was probably an act.

She looked up at him, leaning on the broom handle. "A conspiracy to ruin my auction, that's what."

"Really?"

She had to hand it to him, his look of concern would have fooled anyone who didn't know better. "Don't play dumb. The firefighters got here early to fill up all the slots, then they cooperated to keep the prices down."

Tony's face fell. "Are you sure? Maybe they came early because everyone wanted a piece of Brady's for themselves. Lots of memories were made here."

"What about the cooperative bidding?"

"Firefighters are loyal to each other. Maybe they just didn't want to bid against each other."

"Or maybe they wanted to wreck my auction."

"Maybe. But I don't think so. Priscilla helped you out, didn't she?"

Julie nodded. "Yeah, she did, sort of. But she's not a firefighter."

"As a matter of fact, she is."

"You're kidding." So much for counting on Priscilla and her friends to patronize the tearoom. If she was one of *them*, she probably would prefer bellying up to the bar at Brady's instead of eating quiche and fruit salad at Belinda's.

"I went through training with her," Tony said, "and she's a lot tougher than she looks. She's also my neighbor and landlady."

The undeniable fondness in his voice made Julie bristle. Nothing was more guaranteed to rile her up than a faithless man. "I see. Does she know you asked me out to dinner?"

Tony grinned. "Jealous?"

"No, I'm not jealous! How could you think—"

"Hey, take it easy. Pris and I are just friends."

"Oh." Now she felt silly. She *had* sounded jealous. No, she'd actually *been* jealous. "What are you doing here, anyway?" Julie asked, unable to keep the sharpness out of her voice. "Come to enjoy the aftermath of the train wreck?"

"I wanted to find out how the auction went."

"Now you know. But don't think a bad auction is going to stop me. My plans for Belinda's are going ahead full steam." She might have to scale down her renovation plans. The chandeliers and the mosaic-tile floor would have to wait. But she'd make this happen somehow.

"I'm sorry. About the auction, I mean."

"Save it. You know you just came in here to gloat." Julie went back to her sweeping. It was tempting to poke him with the broom handle, but she'd probably end up being charged with assault. No, the classy owner of a classy tearoom would just ignore her detractors and wait for them to go away.

"You've had a long morning. Why don't you let me take you out to lunch?" Tony asked.

"No, thank you. Why don't you go home and enjoy your new shuffleboard table? I bet Priscilla would play with you."

"I told you, Priscilla's just a friend. But I do think it's cute that you're jealous."

"For the last time, I'm not…" She stopped and made herself calm down. The smile on Tony's face did little to lower her blood pressure, however. He certainly had his nerve showing her that sexy grin when she was in such a foul mood.

She'd already had one career ruined because of a man and she was determined to learn from her mistakes.

"I want you to leave now," she said. "You're not welcome." She picked up a stray piece of broken glass, intending to toss it in the trash, and somehow she managed to cut herself. "Ouch. I'm blaming this on you, too."

"Let me see." He grabbed her hand and inspected the cut. "Damn, that's no little scratch." He led her to the sink behind the bar and ran cold water over her hand. She was acutely aware of the feeling of his hand holding hers, the faint smell of soap and shaving cream and the commanding way he took charge of the situation.

He looked at the cut again. "You should get stitches. I'll drive you to—"

"No, thanks. It'll be fine."

But the cut between her thumb and forefinger hurt like the dickens and it was bleeding at an alarming rate.

"It'll never stop bleeding," Tony said.

"I don't have insurance," she admitted. She'd declined the expensive COBRA health-insurance policy Bailey-Davidson's was legally required to offer when she left employment there. And while she'd checked into some other policies, she hadn't actually gotten around to signing on the dotted line.

Stupid. Irresponsible. She just had too much to do, and some things had fallen between the cracks.

"At least let me walk you across the street. The fire station has first aid."

"The fire station? You guys would probably prefer it if I bled to death." Which was what just might happen if she didn't do something. She'd soaked through three paper towels already.

Tony took offense. "Hey, maybe the firefighters are a little ticked off about losing Brady's, but that doesn't mean they wouldn't do their jobs. They take this stuff seriously."

Julie realized she was being unreasonable. "All right. But if I end up with gangrene, that's your fault, too."

The bar was empty now. Julie gave Tony her keys. He locked the door for her while she put pressure on her cut and then he solicitously walked her across the busy street, his arm around her waist.

She couldn't pretend she was unaffected by the care he gave her. Only minutes earlier she'd wanted to assault him with her broom handle. But now her feelings were quite different.

Hormones, she reminded herself. She couldn't afford to let herself get distracted by hormones. He was a cute guy, so what? Trey was a cute guy, too, and look where her attraction to him had gotten her.

Unemployed and living above a bar.

The reception Julie got at the fire station was cool at first—until they realized she was injured. Then the firefighters couldn't move fast enough to help her. They cleaned the cut with some brown antiseptic, which stung so severely it brought tears to her eyes, then skillfully applied a butterfly bandage. When they were done, she was no longer bleeding.

"I wouldn't use that hand for a couple of days,"

a firefighter named Carl warned her, "or you'll open it up again. You really should have stitches."

"I'll be careful. And thank you."

"Hmph," he said. "If you were really grateful, you'd open Brady's back up."

"Okay, I'm out of here."

"Where you going?" Tony asked.

"Back to work. I have a tearoom to renovate."

"Have you eaten?"

Breakfast was such a distant memory that she had no idea what she'd eaten. And it was past lunchtime. Between lack of sleep, exhaustion, blood loss and her empty stomach, she was swaying on her feet.

"I'm taking you home and feeding you," he said without waiting for an answer.

She wanted to object but found she didn't have the strength. Fine. She'd let him take her home. If he had food in his fridge, she was all for it. "Just know this—I'll be watching, so no trying to poison me."

"I'm not trying to kill you, Julie," he said as if she'd been serious. "I have *much* more interesting plans for you."

She should have been put off by his innuendo. Instead, a shiver of anticipated pleasure rippled through her body, and she realized she should have turned down that lunch invitation. Now it was too late.

"I can drive you if you're feeling too shaky to walk," Tony said, and his concern nearly did Julie in.

"I'm fine, really. You said it was only a block." But she had reason to regret being so stoic as they made their way down Jefferson in the broiling August heat. She had to focus, to put one foot in front of the other and not trip on the cracked sidewalk.

Fortunately Willomet Avenue was lined with live oak trees, planted by some forward-thinking urban pioneer several decades earlier. The slow-growing trees were now a respectable size, providing shade from the sun. Julie breathed a sigh of relief, feeling enough improved that she could appreciate the historic district's quaint, brightly painted homes. Though the area still had some houses in sad shape, most of them had been lovingly restored.

When Tony took Julie's elbow and gently guided her up the front walk of a house painted in three shades of blue toward the end of the block, she saw that his was one of the larger, nicer homes on the street. She'd once thought she'd like to live in an elaborate Victorian home, but the cleaner, sleeker lines of this early-twentieth-century house made it appealing.

"Pretty house," she couldn't resist commenting.

"Thanks. I can't take much credit. Priscilla has gone a little nuts fixing up the place. She owns the house and lives upstairs, but she rents the downstairs unit to me."

"The flowers are beautiful."

"Now those I can take credit for. The yard is all mine."

It looked great. The lush green grass was neatly trimmed, while holly bushes and geraniums dressed up the front yard and lined the porch railings.

Julie could see herself living in this neighborhood. She'd always thought she was a Park Cities girl at heart, but this neighborhood would be so convenient. As soon as Belinda's Tearoom started making money, she could think about upgrading her living arrangements.

"So you garden on your days off?"

"Women garden. I do yard work."

The inside of Tony's house was nothing special, from a decorating standpoint. It was furnished almost sparsely, with simple, unpretentious wood furniture and a rug here and there over the oak-plank floors. But Julie had to admit she liked the feel of the place. With the high ceilings, spacious rooms and dark wood, it was a cool oasis on this sizzling day. It proclaimed a certain comfort. She could feel at home here and put her feet up.

Not at all like Trey's home. She remembered when she'd first seen it, she'd been afraid to touch anything.

Tony pulled off his Texas Rangers cap and stuck it in his back pocket. "Let's go see what we can scare up in the kitchen." He led her past a living room with some puffy furniture—not the latest style but comfortable-looking.

In the kitchen, Tony opened the fridge and started pulling out packages and jars. "How about a sandwich? I have turkey, bologna, salami, some leftover meatballs...."

"It all sounds good." Her stomach rumbled. "Anything." He could have offered her cat food and it would have sounded appealing.

He pulled out a chair for her at the kitchen table. "You sit and relax. You might want to hold your hand up above your heart so it won't throb. Does it hurt?" His concern seemed genuine. Maybe she'd been too hard on him.

"It's not bad."

He fixed them both hot meatball sandwiches and poured tall glasses of Coke. Julie tore into her lunch as if she hadn't eaten in weeks. Just as Tony was about to sit down, though, someone knocked at the kitchen door and he went to open it. Priscilla stood there, dressed in shorts and a Dallas Fire Rescue tank top. She held out a small basket. "Tony, there's a big yellow-jacket nest on my balcony. I know it's girlie of me not to deal with it myself, but I'm allergic to wasp stings. Can you get rid of it?"

"I just sat down to lunch."

"They're coming into my apartment," Priscilla said. "I brought you some of my mom's fudge-raspberry-mousse croquettes as a bribe." She held the basket so Tony could smell the chocolate.

"The sandwich will be here when you get back," Julie said, taking pity on Priscilla. After the termites, she couldn't help but be sympathetic with anyone having problems involving bugs—particularly yellow jackets. Their stings were extremely painful, not to mention life-threatening for someone with an allergy.

Priscilla looked past Tony. "Oh, I'm sorry. I didn't know you had company."

"It's okay," Julie said. "Tony just saved me from bleeding to death, so he's in savior mode."

"All right, I'll take care of the wasps," Tony said. He fished out some bug spray from under the sink. "Priscilla, you stay here. I don't want you getting stung."

"Gladly." She slipped into the kitchen, put her basket on the table and sat in the chair Tony had just left. "Is this a meatball sandwich? Tony makes the best meatballs." And she took a bite. "Mmm. Oh, Julie, what happened to your hand?"

"I cut it on broken glass. That's why I'm here, actually. Tony seems to think it's his sworn duty to play doctor and feed me simply because he was standing there when it happened."

Priscilla laughed. "That's a firefighter for you." And she took another bite of Tony's sandwich.

"Did Lorraine Garner actually bake those with her own hands?" Julie studied the beautiful and dainty pastries, impressed. Priscilla's mother was well known for her baked goods. If you got a basket of cookies or a cake from the Garners for the holidays, you were considered blessed. Lorraine Garner indicated who was in and out of favor—not just with her but with the elite of the city—by who was chosen and who was neglected on that holiday-basket list. Invitations to share food at her home were even more highly desired.

Mrs. Davidson, Trey's mother, had been snubbed last Christmas.

"You know my mother?" Priscilla asked.

"I know *of* her. I haven't actually had the pleasure of meeting her. But I did taste one of her chocolate truffles once, at the home of a friend. Unbelievable."

"I'll tell her you said so. Unfortunately, I didn't inherit any of my mother's culinary skills."

"I'm not much like my parents either," Julie said. She had no idea where she and Belinda had gotten their drive and ambition. Not from their father, who had lost a leg to diabetes and had done nothing to rehabilitate himself, preferring to sit in his wheelchair all day and watch TV. Not from their mother, who worked hard but was content with a dead-end job at a dry cleaner's so long as she could come home to her nightly beer, her crocheting and her tabloid newspapers.

They weren't bad people, just worn down by hard lives. Now that Julie was older, she understood how hard they'd worked to keep their heads above water. She wanted to make sure they were taken care of as they grew older.

The tearoom could help her do that.

"You know, you look awfully familiar," Priscilla said. "Did you go to Highland Park?"

Not hardly. Normally, Julie was a bit cagey about her humble roots. But since she didn't sense an ounce of pretense in Priscilla, she felt compelled to open up. "No, I went to Aaron Burr High." Everyone knew it was a rough high school, both in terms of academics and safety.

Priscilla didn't react, though she had to wonder how a girl from the Grove would have come to move in the same circles as a friend of her mother's.

"You probably saw me at Bailey-Davidson's," Julie said. "I used to work there."

"Oh, yeah! I remember—" Then she stopped short, and Julie could almost see the wheels turning in her head as she struggled to remember some snippet of gossip, trying to put the pieces together. Trey's family, determined that their precious son wouldn't be tainted by scandal, had told everyone that Julie had called off the wedding for unknown reasons. But Trey himself had hinted that Julie had experienced some sort of mental breakdown. "I remember seeing you at Lochinvar's."

"Yes, that's right," Julie said, relieved.

Priscilla took another bite of Tony's sandwich. By now it was half gone. But Julie couldn't really blame her. Her own sandwich was delicious, and she was feeling a hundred percent better. Her head was no longer swimming, her hand didn't hurt quite so much and she was relaxed for the first time in days.

And she liked Priscilla, even if she was a firefighter and in the enemy camp. She seemed so effortlessly classy but friendly, too. That kind of class got into your pores when you were a child, Julie theorized. No matter how hard she tried, no matter how many fashion and decorating magazines she studied, she would never achieve the aura that Priscilla just naturally radiated.

Maybe she could sway Priscilla to her side.

Surely someone with her background could appreciate what Julie wanted to do with the tearoom.

"This house is very nice," Julie said, feeling a change of subject was in order. "I really like the clean, streamlined feel." She couldn't help again comparing it to Trey's house, where elaborate detail was almost a religion. There, every surface was covered with expensive knickknacks. Once, Julie had accidentally broken a small dog figurine. Trey had swept up the shards and assured Julie not to worry about it, but Mrs. Davidson, who'd been there at the time, hadn't been able to resist informing Julie that the figurine was a collectible worth several thousand dollars. Julie had almost fainted.

She didn't think there were any two-thousand-dollar china dogs in this house. She felt comfortable here. In fact, though a few minutes ago she'd protested that she didn't have time to come here for lunch, she now found herself wanting to linger. She was tired of the smell of stale beer and cigarette smoke, which she'd been inhaling for the past week as she'd prepared for the auction. Even after much cleaning, the smells remained in small pockets of Brady's—like when she opened a long-unused drawer, for example.

Tony's place, in contrast, now smelled like meatball sandwiches. But when they'd first walked in, she'd been aware of citrus furniture polish. She loved that fragrance. She even wore a citrus perfume.

"Thanks," Priscilla said. "There's still a lot to be done."

"Do you think Tony's okay?" Julie asked. "He's been gone a while."

"I think he's staying outside on purpose. He wants us to bond, woman to woman, so I can convince you how important Brady's Tavern is to the community and talk you into keeping it just as it was."

Julie sighed. "I appreciate your honesty. And I sympathize with the loss of a place where everyone felt comfortable. But *I* wouldn't have felt comfortable there."

Priscilla finished off Tony's sandwich. "I guess I should make another one of these. How did he do it?"

"He just put some meatballs and cheese on a roll and stuck it in the microwave."

"Okay, I can do that." Priscilla went to work. "I sometimes felt a little uncomfortable at Brady's," she admitted. "And secretly—" she dropped her voice to a whisper "—I'm thrilled you're opening a tearoom."

"You are?"

"Someplace quiet and pleasant where I can get a salad and a glass of wine and not have to listen to loud country music and breathe cigarette smoke in the process. I liked Brady's and I confess I did hang out there. It was fun, and playing darts and shuffleboard helped me to fit in with the guys. But sometimes things change, and change isn't always bad."

"Exactly. I'm so glad you understand."

"But I did want to talk to you about something else." She hesitated, then plunged ahead. "Tony."

"Oh, Tony." Julie waved a dismissive hand, though her heart beat a little faster at the mention of his name. "I can handle Tony. I'm immune to his charm. I just got rid of one man, so I sure don't need another. I might never need another."

"Small world. I got rid of one not too long ago, too."

Oh, it was so, so tempting to tell Priscilla what a skunk Trey Davidson was. But she'd promised the Davidsons not to spread it around.

"I found out he wasn't being totally honest with me." Which was the excuse she had settled on. It wasn't a lie, but it wasn't the whole truth either.

"I'm sorry. Guys can be real jerks. But Tony isn't one of them. The fact is, he likes you. He *really* likes you."

Again Julie's heart quivered. No, no, no, she wasn't going to listen to this. "Tony seems like a nice guy," she said noncommittally.

"He's an exceptionally nice guy. One of the rare ones. You're angry with all the firefighters right now for what they did at your auction, and I don't blame you. But fixing the bidding wasn't Tony's idea. He didn't even know about it, I'm sure. He might want the old Brady's back, but he would never hurt someone else to get his way. That's just not Tony's style."

Julie said nothing. She didn't know what to believe.

"Just promise me you'll be gentle with him. Don't hurt him."

"What? Excuse me? He's totally against me trying to live my life, my dream, and I'm supposed to worry about hurting him?"

"I know this won't make sense to you right now, but at some point it will. Just promise me you'll remember this conversation. Because no matter what it might look like on the outside right now, I predict Tony Veracruz is going to fall in love with you."

Chapter Five

Julie nearly spit out her drink, but somehow she managed to swallow without choking. "Love? Are you kidding me?" She wasn't sure men were even capable of love. Lust, yes. She would never completely understand Trey's reasons for wanting to marry her, but lust had been a part of it. She also suspected he'd appreciated her utter devotion to him. She'd been so in awe of him, maybe he'd thought she would be a doormat and let him have his way in everything. But she knew now his motives had had little to do with love.

"I'm not kidding." Priscilla didn't add anything else.

Feeling awkward now, Julie drained the rest of her cola. "I really do have to go. I appreciate the lunch and the conversation. More than you know." Ever since her breakup with Trey, she'd felt isolated, with only Belinda for commiseration. Most of her friends had been Trey's friends, and they'd naturally sided with him.

Today, for the first time in a long time, she'd felt welcomed. Odd that it would be firefighters who made her feel that way.

She stood and took her dishes to the sink, considering how she might slip out without having to see Tony again. But even as she decided that would be too rude, Tony returned, smiling victoriously. "Those were some ticked-off wasps. But they're gone now."

"You sure?"

"Sure, I'm—hey, what happened to my sandwich?"

"It was getting cold, so I put it in the microwave," Priscilla said quickly. "Thanks, Tony. See ya!" And she escaped.

Tony shook his head and laughed. "She's a piece of work. And whatever she told you about me, it's not true. That bucket of water we dumped on her from the second floor didn't hurt her at all, no matter what she says."

Julie grinned. If Tony had any idea what Priscilla had *really* said about him, he'd probably flip. "Priscilla had many interesting things to say about you—none of them having to do with a bucket of water."

"Then forget what I just said. I would never dump a bucket of water on an unsuspecting colleague."

"Uh-huh. Tony, I really have to go."

"Don't you want to go out and see my puppy? His name's Dino, and he's even cuter than Bluto."

"Another time maybe." Julie was surprised at how much she wanted to stay and loll away the afternoon with Tony and his Dalmatian pup. What was wrong with her? She had work to do, a tearoom to renovate, numbers to crunch, advertising and promotion to dream up. She absolutely did not have time to loll.

"I'll walk you back to Brady's, then."

"Belinda's."

"Whatever."

"Belinda's. Say it. Belinda's Tearoom."

"I just can't. I would be a traitor to my kind."

"Fine. I'll walk alone."

He screwed up his face. "Belinda's Tearoom. There, I said it." Then he did walk her back to the bar. And when she reached the front door, he tried to steal a kiss.

She ducked her head, refusing to let his lips make contact, no matter how badly she wanted that kiss herself. Weak, weak, weak.

"Tony, this wasn't a date."

"It felt like one." He took a step closer, backing her against the door before she could get the stubborn lock to turn. "I've been thinking about kissing you ever since I watched you take a bite of that sandwich. The way you closed your mouth around it, then sighed with appreciation…"

"Tony, really!" This guy was just too much. Equating eating a sandwich with a kiss? Ridiculous!

"Just one kiss and then I'll leave you alone."

"Forever?"

"Now you wound me. You'd be sad if you never saw me again."

She wanted to tell Tony that nothing would give

her more pleasure than to rid her life of him and all firefighters. But it was such a lie she couldn't say it. She *would* be sad if she never saw him again. He'd gotten under her skin.

Now he had a hand on either side of her, trapping her between his arms. "Look me in the eye and tell me you don't want to kiss me."

She looked him straight in the eye. But again the words wouldn't come. Because all she could think about was his mouth and how she'd imagined it would feel against hers. And how it would feel now...

"You can't say it, can you?"

"I don't want to—" That was all she managed to get out before his lips caught hers midsentence and her world tipped on its axis. Before she knew what was happening, her arms had slid around his neck and she was straining to press her body against his, so warm and hard and masculine. And the way he smelled—like soap and laundry detergent, with a hint of musk and maybe a trace of smoke. His mouth was insistent but gentle, too, teasing responses from her rather than demanding them.

He was getting exactly what he wanted. She felt as if her bones were melting.

Only a honk from a passing motorist brought her back to her senses. She forced herself to pull away, to put some steel in her backbone and stop this nonsense.

Tony obviously sensed her change of mood and gave her a parting nibble at the corner of her mouth.

"Will you please stop kissing me?"

"I gave you a chance to say you didn't want it."

She ducked under his arm and out of his light embrace. "I tried. You didn't give me enough time."

"All day wouldn't have been enough time."

She finally got the lock to turn and opened the door. She stepped inside and turned, effectively blocking the doorway. "You're pretty sure of yourself."

He shrugged, and a fleeting ghost of doubt flitted across his handsome features. "You might be surprised."

"Goodbye, Tony." She forced herself to shut the door. She could not let him distract her or sway her and she would not feel sympathy toward him and his firefighter friends for losing their hangout. She had to keep focused on her goal. Security for her parents. An education for her sister. A place for her to belong. A place that would prove to Trey just how much she didn't need his money or his influence.

Perhaps most important, she had to stay in control of her own destiny and never again pin her hopes on someone who had the power to send all her plans crashing down around her ears.

CAR ACCIDENT. VEHICLE *on fire. People trapped inside.* Those were words to strike fear in any firefighter's heart—or, more accurately, not fear but an adrenaline rush that quickened the step and put more speed and purpose into his actions.

Engine 59 was less than a minute away. Tony, on paramedic duty, was right behind the engine in the "box"—the ambulance. A plume of black smoke from the fire led them straight to the accident at the busy intersection of Twelfth Street and Hampton, where traffic was now tied up in knots. Both engine and ambulance drove up on the sidewalk to get through.

When they reached the scene, things looked bad. Two cars, one on fire, civilians screaming and running around trying to get the doors open on the burning car and then retreating quickly from the intense heat. Tony wanted nothing more than to charge into the blaze and get to the people in the burning car. Training went right out the window as he started to do just that, but Lt. McCrae yelled at him to get back.

In seconds, McCrae and Priscilla had a small booster line in hand and were using a fog to attack the flames that came out from under the hood. They beat back the blaze just enough that Ethan could get in and get the driver's door open, and that was Tony's signal to go into action, finally. The car had just one occupant, a teenage boy behind the wheel.

"He's alive," Ethan announced, his relief evident.

Tony, who'd learned to keep a pocketknife on hand, cut the seat belt. He did his best to support the boy's neck and head while Kevin and Ethan got him onto a backboard. Once he was out of the car, Tony put a C-collar on him and they got him onto a stretcher.

Meanwhile, Otis got the hood open with a crowbar. Flames whooshed out, then just as suddenly disappeared as the hose line found the source of the blaze and extinguished it.

Tony's patient was bleeding from a cut on his head, where he'd hit the steering wheel. The old car didn't have air bags, but his seat belt had probably prevented a more serious injury. He was breathing but unconscious, whether from inhaling smoke and fumes or from a concussion it was hard to tell.

Back in the box Kevin drove while Tony tended to their patient. "BP one hundred over forty-two, respiration fourteen," he reported to Bio-Tel, the service that had a doctor on hand to provide medical advice. "Both pupils respond to light." He put pressure on the cut, which was bleeding profusely, then started an IV as the ambulance jerked and swayed and bumped its way to the closest trauma unit at Methodist Medical Center.

Once the basics were covered, Tony found the kid's wallet in a back pocket and reported the name and age. The poor kid hadn't had his license more than a couple of months.

Minutes later, the boy was delivered into the capable hands of the ER doctors. Tony took a deep breath and waited for the metabolic crash that inevitably came after a life-or-death sprint to the hospital. All that adrenaline, then nothing. He filled out the required paperwork, reported to the dispatcher that they were clear, then prayed for another call.

But nothing else came in, so he and Kevin returned to the station, where Tony's gaze was inevitably drawn to Brady's—or what used to be Brady's. The weathered sign was gone now.

For the past two weeks Tony and the rest of the firefighters had been watching various workers tromp in and out of the old tavern—floor sanders, electricians, plumbers and thankfully even an exterminator. Today, the outside of the building was getting a sandblasting, years of grime disappearing to reveal the true creamy color of the bricks.

The only thing worse than watching Brady's disappear before their eyes was catching glimpses of Julie, striding to and from her little blue Mini Cooper, always with purpose and determination in her step. Sometimes she carried various supplies with her—tools, wallpaper books, tile samples. Sometimes just a briefcase bulging with papers.

Tony had to admit she was making it happen. She had a plan and she was carrying it out with the precision of a military general. He wanted to get inside and see what she was doing, but so far, every time he'd wandered by on his days off, the door to the former bar had either been locked or barred with yellow caution tape and a sign indicating it was a hard-hat zone. In two weeks, he hadn't once managed to catch Julie and talk to her.

But she was always in his thoughts. A few days ago someone had casually asked him if he'd heard from Daralee, and he'd had to struggle a few seconds to even remember who Daralee was. All he could think about was Julie. And as before, the only thing that took his mind off his romantic troubles was work and more work. The slow shifts were torture.

The only good news was he was spending so much time at the weight bench, where he had a good view from the window overlooking the building across the street, that he was building some new muscles.

Finally, early the following morning, just as he was getting off his shift, he saw Julie's car drive up and park at a meter in front of her building.

Though he was grimy from putting out a kitchen fire and he hadn't had a chance to shower yet, he didn't delay. He sprinted across the street and caught her just as she was getting out of her car.

Startled, she looked from side to side for an escape route before finally resigning herself to a conversation. "Hello, Tony."

"Morning. You've been avoiding me."

"I don't have time to argue with you about my tearoom. I have things to do, places to go, people to meet." She headed resolutely for the front door, keys in hand. But she stopped before she reached it, perhaps remembering what had happened the last time he accompanied her toward that door.

"Tony, I'm really in a rush."

"What's up? Anything I can help with?"

"Help? Ha. You only have one thing in mind, and it's not helping me. You'd like to stop me from opening Belinda's. And I'm not going to let you."

"You're partly right. I do have only one thing on my mind. But it has nothing to do with your tearoom."

Her face flushed pink and she looked away. "If that's true, than there's even more reason to avoid you. I don't have time for your nonsense."

"You didn't think that kiss was nonsense. Admit it, Julie, you've hardly been able to think of anything else." If the kiss had affected her the way it affected him, that was how it worked.

She still wouldn't meet his gaze, which gave him some hope that he was right. She wasn't made of ice.

While her guard was down he took the keys from her hand and strolled toward the building, and she had no choice but to follow.

Tony opened the door and held it for her to enter. She did so quickly, but not before he felt the heat of her body and caught a whiff of her citrus scent. If he didn't have his way with this woman soon, he was going to expire from the wanting.

He followed her into the darkness and waited for his eyes to adjust, but then Julie turned on the lights and he got his first really good look at Belinda's Tearoom.

It was a strange sensation looking around at the changes, because the place still felt like Brady's— but not quite. All of the tables and chairs, neon signs and games were gone. The floor had been sanded bare.

The most dramatic change, though, was that the far back room of the bar had been walled off. Anyone who didn't know the history of the place would swear that wall had always been there, it blended so seamlessly with the rest of the space.

"What happened to the back room?" he asked.

"That's where the kitchen is."

It was depressing to realize the old Brady's was gone for good. But Tony wasn't giving up yet. If he could just spend some time with Julie, he was sure he could get her to understand why the tearoom was a bad idea. "You've made good progress," he said finally.

That obviously wasn't the observation she'd been hoping for from him, because she frowned. "You can't do better than that?"

"It's a big, empty space. I'm sure somehow you'll make it look like a tearoom. But it won't be Brady's, and I can feel the Ghosts of Brady's Past hanging out in the corners, cringing."

He expected her to shoot back a retort. But instead she hugged herself and shivered. "I wish you hadn't said that. You know, I'm living in my uncle's apartment and sometimes I think I can feel him there. Disapproving. I know it's my imagination, but after everything you've told me about Brady—about how generous he was and how everyone called him a friend—I'm feeling bad about destroying the place he helped to create."

Then, as if just realizing what she'd admitted, she suddenly turned all business. "Would you look at the mess those floor guys left! They were supposed to clean up everything before they took off yesterday." She started picking up discarded scraps of wood and bent nails.

Tony hadn't in a million years expected her to

make such an honest admission. He found himself wanting to sympathize, sharing her need to fulfill her dream. But he hardened his heart. The guys wouldn't speak to him for a week if they knew.

"It's not too late, you know. You could still make this a bar, and it wouldn't have to be grungy like before. Have you been to that new place in Bishop Arts?" He grabbed a broom and started sweeping up sawdust because it didn't feel right just standing there, doing nothing, while she worked. "It's really fancy. They serve those multicolored fruity martinis for eight bucks a pop. You don't think there's a heckuva profit margin there?"

"Turn Brady's into a martini bar?" Julie made a face. "I don't think Uncle Brady would like that any better. Besides, I told you, I don't know anything about running a bar." She paused and stared at him suspiciously. "You guys would freak if I turned this place into some high-priced beautiful-people bar. Is this some new game you're playing, using reverse psychology or something?"

Tony shrugged as he found a dustpan. "It doesn't have to be that fancy. I miss Brady's. Everybody does. But I like you and I want to see you succeed with this venture and make a profit. A bar is going to do better than a tearoom."

For about a half second her amber eyes glowed a little warmer, and he thought she believed him. But then she dropped her protective shutters into place, just as if she'd dropped the blinds on her window as a barrier between them.

"I do want to make enough money so that I can send Belinda to college and help out my parents."

"And that's a good thing. I fully support that."

She grabbed a trash bag that was already half-full and started pitching lumber scraps into it. Tony dumped a load of sawdust in, too.

"You smell like smoke," she said.

"I just got back from a kitchen fire. I was on my way home to shower when I saw you." He tied up the ends of the trash bag, which was now full. He'd been thinking about kissing her again, but she'd reminded him of his unkempt state. "Where's your trash?"

"It's back here." She led him behind the bar to a storage room, where a huge plastic garbage bin was already overflowing with refuse. "Oh, shoot, just drop that bag anywhere. I need to take my trash out to the alley. So what happened with the kitchen fire?"

"It was at Norma's Café—you know, that diner over on Davis?"

"Everyone knows Norma's, even people who don't live in Oak Cliff. Best chicken-fried steak in town—so I hear."

"But your lips never touch fried food, I take it."

"I wouldn't say that," she admitted. "I love Norma's. Was the fire bad?"

"Nah, just a little grease. They'll be back open by tomorrow."

"Oh, that's good."

"Norma's is your competition. I thought you'd want to see them closed."

She seemed disturbed by his suggestion. "Is that the impression I've given you? Tony, number one, Norma's and Belinda's appeal to completely different clientele. But number two, I would never wish a fire or anything else bad on anyone. Ever."

"You're right. I'm sorry, that wasn't fair." Tony helped Julie wrestle with the trash bin. "I can handle this if you'll get that last bag. Anyway, the fire was out in about thirty seconds. But I got a little steam burn. See?" He showed her a bright red crescent on his wrist. "Rookie mistake. I put my gloves on too quick and left a gap."

She felt an urge to kiss the red mark on his arm as she shook her head. "I don't know how you do it. Placing yourself in danger, saving people's lives. Don't you find it hard? What about those fires that aren't so easy? Or when people are seriously hurt, even killed. Your job makes my plan to open a tearoom seem…I don't know…silly and insignificant."

She tied the top of the bag in a knot and walked it toward the back door, which led to the alley.

Tony laid a hand on her arm, halting her. "Tearooms aren't silly. The world needs tearooms. Just like it needs neighborhood bars."

She rolled her eyes. "I was starting to like you a little bit."

He grinned and wrestled the trash bin out the back door, then held the door open for her.

"You don't have to be such a gentleman, you know."

"Can't help it. Anyway, you're still injured." He

pointed to her bandaged hand. "You shouldn't be doing all this heavy work." He'd noticed that she had her hand wrapped up in new bandages, rather inexpertly, but she seemed to be using it okay.

"It's almost healed now. Doesn't hurt at all." She opened the Dumpster lid and he heaved the bag inside. They both turned back as the lid slammed shut—and froze in their steps.

Someone had spray painted a message on the back wall in three-foot-high letters: *Bring Brady's back or else.*

Chapter Six

Julie's hands flew to her mouth as she took in the graffiti.

Tony felt sick.

"Well, that's just lovely," Julie said finally. "Did you get what you came for? Was my reaction suitably dramatic? Would it make a better story if I fell to the ground in tears?"

"Julie, I don't know anything about this." He reached out to touch her shoulder, knowing how hurt and frustrated she must feel at being attacked, but she stepped away from him.

"Don't touch me."

"I didn't do this."

"But you know who did."

"No. I have no idea." But he sure would love to find out. Applying a bit of romance to sway Julie's thinking wasn't exactly aboveboard, but it wasn't criminal. This was way over the line. If he found out who did it, the guy was going to be in a world of pain.

Julie trembled with outrage. Tony wanted to help her, comfort her. But his comfort was about as welcome as an electric shock.

"I can fix this," he said. "Kids spray paint this wall all the time. Brady just painted over the graffiti."

"*You're* not fixing anything. *I'll* fix it. And you can put the word out. If I find out who did this, I'll make his life miserable."

That went double for Tony, but he doubted Julie was in any mood to believe him. Words were cheap. He was going to have to *do* something to prove he wasn't her adversary.

"I'll get to the bottom of this," he said.

Less than a minute later he was across the street, back at Station 59, where the guys from the A shift were attending to their morning rituals—cooking breakfast, drinking coffee, checking out the day's news. He knew a couple of them but only casually, so he started by shaking hands and introducing himself.

"What, you just can't get enough of this place on your own shift?" one of the men ribbed him.

"I was just across the street at Brady's, talking to the new owner," he said. "Someone spray painted graffiti on her back wall."

A couple of the guys applauded and another whistled. "Good job. Was it you?"

"No, it wasn't me." His strenuous objection earned him a few curious stares. "I know everyone's ticked off about what's happening to Brady's. But don't y'all think committing malicious mischief against Julie is going a little far?"

"Julie, is it?" asked a lanky lieutenant. "Whose side are you on, Rookie?"

Tony sighed. *Rookie.* It had been a while since he'd had to deal with that moniker. Ethan, Priscilla and Tony had filled the vacancies at Station 59 caused by the deaths of three firefighters killed in the warehouse fire set by the serial arsonist, and resentments had run strong their first few weeks. But the three rookies had proved themselves. They'd all been in fires, they'd done their duty and gradually their colleagues had come to give them grudging respect.

Suddenly Tony was green again.

"I'm not on anyone's side," he said. "I'm trying harder than anyone to convince her to reopen Brady's just as it was. But she has definite ideas about what she wants to do with the bar, and no harassment is going to change her mind."

"So are you accusing someone here of painting this chick's wall?" one of the guys demanded.

"I'm not accusing anyone. I have no idea who did it. But if you know who did it, I hope you'll tell that person he's not helping matters."

"How do you know it was a 'he'?" the lieutenant asked. "Maybe it was a siren sister."

And maybe it was the Easter bunny. But Tony doubted it was anybody but a fellow firefighter. Maybe a cop, but probably not.

"I'm just saying it's not helping, that's all." He decided to cut his losses and get the hell out of there before the mood got any more hostile. He needed a shower and some sleep. Then he was going to buy some paint and get rid of the ugly words on Julie's wall, whether she wanted his help or not.

WHEN JULIE STEPPED OUT into the alley that afternoon to toss yet another bag of garbage into the Dumpster, she was surprised to encounter a man on a ladder painting her back wall. Her immediate reaction was to jump to the conclusion she'd caught her graffiti artist red-handed—until she realized the man was Tony, and he was painting over the last of the hurtful words with a nice neutral beige that almost matched the natural color of the bricks.

He turned when he heard the door and grinned. "Hi, there."

"Tony, I told you not to bother."

"I make a habit of doing what I'm told not to do. It gets me in a lot of trouble."

"The really irksome thing about you is you seem to *like* trouble."

"Most firefighters do, I guess."

She watched silently as Tony obliterated the last of the awful red letters. Her relief at seeing the graffiti disappear felt like a cool gust of wind.

"Tony, why are you doing this?"

"Because I feel responsible," he answered without hesitation. "I don't know who painted your wall, but it must have been a firefighter. Whoever he is, though, he doesn't represent all of us. I think you should know that not all firefighters would stoop so low as to break the law. We're not all bad."

"I never thought all firefighters were bad." But maybe she had. Maybe she had generalized, assuming things about Tony based on his occupation, the way people had once assumed she was unworthy or even stupid because she didn't wear the right shoes and didn't speak with the right inflections.

She felt a little guilty when she realized that. "It looks very nice. Thank you." Truthfully she'd had no idea when she was going to get around to painting over the graffiti. She hadn't wanted to waste any of her precious renovation budget on something so stupid, so she'd planned to do the painting herself. Now she didn't have to worry.

He smiled again. "You're welcome."

She felt herself softening toward Tony. Though she knew that was a dangerous development, she couldn't seem to help herself. "Come on inside and get something to drink. You can sit at the bar and pretend you're at Brady's."

"It won't seem like Brady's unless you're serving warm beer. And you'd have to be wearing a mini-skirt and halter top, like Brady's waitresses did."

"Not in this lifetime. You'll have to settle for cold lemonade and faded jeans."

His gaze traveled in a leisurely path down her body to look at those jeans, and her face warmed. If another guy did that, she would feel affronted. But Tony's look was so…appreciative. It made her feel beautiful and sexy rather than insulted by his boldness.

She was about to step back into the building when something caught her eye, a small red spot on her beige brick wall. She stepped closer to get a better look, while Tony cleared his throat.

"Um, you weren't supposed to notice that."

It was a little red heart, only a couple of inches across, painted on one brick. Beside it Tony had signed his initials.

"See, my original plan was to paint over the graffiti and move on before you saw me. So it would be a big surprise. But then I decided to leave a clue."

"So I could thank you."

"I was secretly hoping you'd be so grateful you'd want to go out with me."

Hell. How was she supposed to respond to that? With his big brown eyes and his earnest manner, she wanted to take him home and feed him like a stray puppy.

And then give him a warm place to sleep. If they ever got around to sleeping.

He did make it pretty hard to stay mad. "Lemonade," she said, strengthening her resolve. He wasn't a puppy, he was a man. A firefighter who hated her tearoom and wanted his dingy old bar back.

Tony opened the door for her, and she had to brush close to him to get inside. He had a knack for making her do that. She couldn't help noticing that he no longer smelled like smoke.

From the small fridge behind the bar she produced a couple of cans of lemonade. But there was no place to sit. Every stick of the old furniture had been sold, and the new tables and chairs she'd ordered wouldn't arrive until the renovations were completed.

Tony solved the problem by vaulting onto the bar. He sat facing out, his legs dangling. "Come on up, the view is fine."

Since she needed a break and didn't want to sit on the floor, she followed his example, sitting just close enough that she could feel the heat radiating off him.

She'd never seen the tearoom from this angle before. It looked enormous. Not quite as big as Lochinvar's, but the size was still intimidating.

"So tell me about your tearoom. What kind of food are you going to serve?"

"I'm still working out all the details, but I'm planning on an eclectic menu. Specialty salads, soups, quiche, then a few heartier seafood and chicken dishes."

"No burgers?"

"No, but there'll be a few sandwiches."

"Ribs?" he asked hopefully.

"Definitely not."

"So no guy food."

"The menu will be designed to appeal primarily to women, but there is no law that says a guy can't eat a salad or a club sandwich."

"What about liquor?"

"Wine only."

He sighed. "You know, you might actually attract a few businessmen if you put some token items on the menu that appeal to men. Steak, chili, burgers, maybe some designer beer—"

"I don't want tables full of noisy men who've been drinking. Then the women won't want to eat here. I want refinement. Quiet conversation. I want my customers to appreciate the decor and the background music. I'm thinking of hiring a harpist to come in once or twice a week during lunch, to really give the place some atmosphere."

Tony groaned.

"You're not scaring me. It's not meant to appeal to you."

"Just how many tea-drinking, itty-bitty-sandwich-eating, harp-music-listening women of leisure do you think live in Oak Cliff?"

"Not necessarily women of leisure. Working women will come here on their lunch break. I intend for the service to be quick."

"Oak Cliff working women won't be able to afford your prices, not on a regular basis."

"You don't even know what my prices are."

"I can guess."

"You're not scaring me," she said again. "I know what I'm doing." Not for the first time since she'd committed herself to this idea, however, she had some doubts. What if Tony was right? What if her concept was just too high-end for this working-class neighborhood?

No, she wasn't going to worry about that. What did Tony know? He didn't have any restaurant experience.

"I'm not trying to scare you," he said. "Honestly. I'm trying to help you attract more customers so you can stay open."

"Stay open?"

"Something like ninety percent of restaurant start-ups close within the first year."

"Now you're scaring me." She'd encountered the statistic before.

He slipped an arm around her and scooted closer. "I'll stop. Tell me more. Will you be open for breakfast?"

"Just lunch, at first. Once I get the hang of that, I'm planning to offer a limited breakfast—pastries, coffee and tea."

"Bagels with cream cheese?" he asked hopefully. "No one around here serves a decent bagel. Crispy on the outside, chewy on the inside…" He nibbled her ear. "I'd be here every morning if you served a good bagel."

"I'm beginning to think what you really want is hot Julie on a platter." The blood rushed to her face. Had she really just said that?

"Mmm, that sounds even better than bagels. I'll be here an hour early for that."

She couldn't believe this guy. He didn't even deny he wanted in her pants! But she also couldn't believe herself. She was sitting here letting him nibble her ear and her neck, making no move to escape. She opened her mouth to tell him to stop, but what he was doing just felt too good.

She reached up a hand to push him away, but then she remembered the little red heart he'd left on her wall and her own heart just melted. Along with a few other strategically placed body parts.

"Tony," she implored, but he ignored her, planting

little kisses along her jaw. Eventually, he reached the corner of her mouth. If he actually kissed her on the lips, she would be a goner. Her body was already clamoring for more Tony. Her breasts strained against her bra, her nipples hard and achy. And the heat building at the core of her being was like a furnace in the basement of an old building, long disused but raging back to life with the touch of a lit match.

Trey had never made her feel quite like this, like a bowl of melting gelatin. Common sense, good judgment and willpower had left the building.

But, honestly, what could happen? They were sitting on a hard wooden bar. Would it hurt to make out? They were already making out. She had her tongue in his mouth—that was making out.

When a loud banging noise finally penetrated her lust-fogged mind, she realized someone was knocking on the door.

"Ignore it," Tony said. His hand was up her shirt, caressing her breast, and she wanted more than anything to do what he said. But she couldn't.

"It's the man here to install my new stove." She was shocked by the breathy croak of her own voice. "I have to let him in."

Reluctantly Tony relinquished his hold. He withdrew slowly but without arguing further.

Julie hopped off the bar, found the shoe she'd dropped and ran for the door, where a man with a handcart waited impatiently. "Thought you were in a hurry to get your kitchen done," he said as she let him in.

"Sorry. I didn't hear you knocking at first." Which was true. Her brain had been so filled with Tony there hadn't been room for anything else. "I'll open the back door for you."

She had no business dallying with Tony. The installer already knew exactly what to do, so she left him to his business. It wasn't as if she didn't have a million other things to attend to. But first she had one little matter to take care of.

Or maybe not so little.

Tony stood with his back against the bar, arms folded, looking just this side of smug. "Lucky we were interrupted."

"Lucky? You're glad?"

"When I make love to you," he said in a low voice, "I don't want it to be on a hard wooden bar. We're going to have a soft bed, rose petals, champagne…."

"Oh, please." Though she couldn't deny the picture he painted had its appeal.

"I want to take you out for a steak dinner," he said, not the slightest deterred by her negative attitude. "Wine, violins, the whole nine yards."

Her mouth watered. She hadn't had any dinner more elaborate than tuna casserole or mac-and-cheese since she and Trey had broken up. "Then you were going to seduce me."

"Make love to you." The way he said it, all soft and sexy, made her skin itch for his touch. How did he do that? One minute she was sure she wanted to sweep him out of the bar, and the next she was drooling to be in his arms again. "I want you to wear your sexiest dress and your highest pair of heels so I can show you off."

Julie walked behind the bar, careful to keep more than an arm's reach away from Tony, and gathered up some cleaning rags that needed washing, stuffing them into a plastic bag. "I'm not a prize poodle."

"Julie, why are you being like this? What's wrong?"

Julie made herself stop and think. She *was* being harsh. And unfair. If a man ran hot and cold as she was doing, it would make her furious.

"I'm sorry, Tony. I know I'm being inconsistent. But having a guy in my life right now—it just won't work." She didn't add that her plans particularly didn't include hooking up with a firefighter. It wasn't that she had anything against Tony or his occupation. In fact, she found it very brave and noble. But it just didn't fit in with the vision she had for her future.

"Why not?"

"Belinda's is taking up a hundred percent of my time and energy right now. Anyway, we don't even know each other." He'd flirted with her, but he hadn't told her anything important about himself.

"So if I don't take you out to dinner tomorrow night, what will you do instead?"

"Sew curtains." The price of custom window treatments was so outrageous that Julie had decided she would have to make her own. She'd sewn her clothes as a teen; it was the only way she'd been able to afford to wear the styles and fabrics that appealed to her. Even when she'd been able to buy high-quality clothing, she'd still occasionally made her own creations, which had earned her many compliments.

No one had ever suspected. But her sewing habit was an embarrassing little secret she'd kept from Trey.

"You can do that?" Tony asked. "That's really talented. And are you going to be sewing curtains every night for the foreseeable future?"

She carried her bag of laundry into the storage room, where an ancient but serviceable washer and dryer occupied one wall. "If I'm not sewing curtains, I'll be painting or sanding or texturing. I'm building a mosaic countertop around the sink in the ladies' room and a stained-glass pane for the window over the door. I have a million projects." She stuffed the dirty rags into the washer, emphasizing how very busy she was.

"So I could bring over a bucket of chicken and help you. I can't sew, but I can sand and paint—I can even do laundry—and you wouldn't have to pay me with anything but your charming company."

She almost said yes. He was so darn cute and he could charm the skin right off a snake. But she made herself shake her head. "Even if I had the time, I'm not ready to date. I just broke up with a guy. It was a couple of weeks before our wedding and I found out…" Her throat still closed up when she thought about it. It had been such a shock. Her whole world had shifted and a new reality had taken over in mere seconds.

She wouldn't be marrying Trey Davidson. She wouldn't be changing her name or moving into Trey's Highland Park home. She was single again. Alone. She hadn't really belonged in that world of privilege. She'd only been a guest, one who could be ejected at the whim of her host.

And eject her Trey had. He was the one who'd cheated and lied, yet somehow he'd managed to blame her and justify his anger toward her.

"He was unfaithful, huh? Bastard."

"Not just unfaithful. He had a child. But the very worst thing was he refused to take responsibility. When he found out she was pregnant, he cranked up the family's legal machine and tried every way possible to get rid of the woman, right down to having her deported."

"Jeez. It's a good thing you didn't marry the guy. But what does that have to do with us?"

"I'm on the rebound."

He shrugged. "So am I. I just broke up with someone, too. We weren't engaged, but it was serious. Well, sort of."

"So we're both on the rebound. Recipe for disaster."

"I can't think of a better way to get over a bad affair than to find love with someone else."

Love? She remembered the strange prediction Priscilla Garner had made, then pushed it out of her mind.

"You see, Tony, I made a mistake. Not just with whom I picked as a partner but why I wanted to be with someone in the first place. I placed my entire future in someone else's hands rather than relying on myself. I need to find out what I can do with my life—on my own."

"So bottom line…you're telling me you just want to be friends?" He pulled a face at that old hackneyed expression, and she couldn't blame him.

But was that what she wanted? Friends? How could she have Tony around as a friend when she was so attracted to him? Could she keep her hands off him? Did she really want to tell Tony to go away and not come back, that she was a loner and wanted to stay that way? Could she take a couple of days to think about it?

But she already knew the answer to that question. If she gave Tony an inch, he'd take a mile. He'd be in her life, in her bed; she would fall in love, and everything would be topsy-turvy until he decided some other woman had something she didn't.

"Just friends."

"Okay, then." He looked sad for a moment, and she almost blurted out that she'd changed her mind. But then he grinned. "You're a really good kisser, anyone ever tell you that?" And without giving her a chance for a comeback, he gave her a two-finger salute and sauntered out the door into the hot afternoon.

Chapter Seven

Tony tried to shake off Julie's rejection as he made the short walk home. Not even the prospect of seeing Jasmine for the first time in two weeks could completely cheer him up, though it helped. She would be here in about an hour, he reckoned. Just enough time to take another shower, then run to the store and buy some of those double-fudge brownies she liked.

Jas was a chocoholic in the making. Tony tried to be a good dad and not let her indulge herself too much, but this was a special occasion. His daughter had been visiting her grandparents in Galveston for the past two weeks—the longest she and Tony had ever been separated.

When he got home with the brownies, he opened a can of fudge icing and frosted them, then put some colored sprinkles on top, because she liked those, too.

As he put on the finishing touches, Priscilla knocked on the back door and let herself in. "Well, aren't you domestic."

"Do you have, like, some sort of specialized food radar? 'Cause I swear, every time I have something good and I'm just about to eat it, you show up."

"Actually, I wanted to ask you if you would quiz me for my test. It's on drugs and drug interactions, poisons, antidotes and overdose protocol. I need help, and Ethan's not home."

Priscilla and Ethan were working toward their paramedic certification, a requirement for all Dallas firefighters. Tony didn't envy them, having to go through a solid year of training while they were still adjusting to the job of fighting fires. Fortunately he'd been a paramedic before he applied to the fire department.

"I wish I could help you study, Pris, but Jasmine will be here any minute. I haven't seen her in two weeks and I want to spend some time with her."

Pris smiled at the mention of Jasmine. Everyone loved her. She was such a sweet, loving, uncomplicated kid. A lot of people said she was like Tony in terms of her personality, which always made him feel proud. But if that was the case, the poor girl was probably in for some heartbreak when she got older.

"So what have you been up to?" Pris asked as she opened the refrigerator. She never came into his kitchen without opening his fridge and swiping something, since her fridge was notoriously empty. Considering she brought him goodies from her mother's kitchen, though, he couldn't complain too bitterly.

"I was painting over some graffiti on the back wall of Brady's. You wouldn't happen to know who's responsible, would you?"

"Don't look at me." She closed the fridge and opened the freezer, finally settling on a cherry Popsicle.

"I just thought maybe you'd heard something. This campaign to stop Julie from opening the tearoom has gotten way out of hand."

"What about you? Have you given up on the cold-blooded-seduction thing?" Pris asked.

Tony sighed. "It's not my style. I tried to stop myself from falling in love with Julie, but I can't just *not* feel anything for her. I mean, she's so…she's just so… Damn, Pris, what am I doing wrong?"

"She's not interested?" Pris asked. "I find that hard to believe. I saw the way she looked at you."

"Yeah, the way a lot of women *look* at me. Apparently I'm okay to look at. Or make out with. In some cases, I'm okay to have sex with. But that's it."

"Oh, Tony. I'm sure that's not true. What happened?"

"Julie gave me the 'just friends' speech. You know the one."

"'The timing's wrong. It's me not you'?"

"That's the one." Tony, having temporarily forgotten the brownies were for Jasmine, took a bite out of one. "She's all into this 'on the rebound' stuff. Her last boyfriend was some jerk who cheated on her, and now she thinks all guys are like him. She won't go out with me. So what did I do wrong?"

"Well, you do come on a little strong."

Tony stopped just as he was about to take another bite. Too strong?

"I mean, don't take this wrong, but I think you might scare a woman to bits because you're so… intense. And persistent."

He thought intensity and persistence were good things.

"Are you in love with Julie?" Priscilla asked suddenly.

"I'm trying not to go there. But I could be. In a big way. I mean, what if she's The One?"

"You think every girl you meet is The One. It's called infatuation. Not that infatuation can't develop into love, but you don't know Julie well enough to have such strong feelings about her. A few weeks ago you were in love with Daralee."

"Now *that* was infatuation."

"But you thought she was The One, didn't you? And I think you scared her off. You did the same thing with Karla."

Karla. He hadn't thought about her in forever. She'd been a secretary at the firefighter school. And, yes, he'd thought she was The One, too.

"And before that—"

"Okay, I get—"

"You see the pattern, right?" Priscilla asked.

"That women break up with me after a few weeks? Yeah, I've got that down."

"Because real, lasting relationships don't build overnight. And most women know that. Maybe they think you're a player. Maybe they don't believe you're sincere. Because frankly, Tony, you're a catch. Any girl would be lucky to have you and keep you. The only thing I can figure out is that you're scaring them away because you're just too damn good to be true."

Tony put the half-eaten brownie aside. His stomach hurt. "You think?"

"I don't know. I've been trying to figure it out. I've also wondered why there's no chemistry between you and me."

"Because we're friends. I'd never want to mess that up."

"So you think you can't be friends and lovers at the same time?"

"I was being friendly to Julie," he argued. "I painted over her graffiti."

"Because you wanted to soften her up. So she'd go to bed with you. And let's face it, you have an even darker ulterior motive. You want to mess up her plans for the tearoom."

"I do want to change her mind, for her own good as well as ours," Tony said. "If she would get to know me better, if she could trust me, maybe she would believe it when I tell her the tearoom thing is a bad idea."

"So you have ulterior motives. Why don't you try being friends, no strings attached?"

"I can't stop wanting her. It's not like a faucet I can turn on and off."

"I know. But here's the deal—if you had an iron-clad guarantee that you and Julie will never, ever get together, would you still want to spend time with her?"

"Yes." That was easy.

"Then do it. Be her friend. Get it fixed in your mind that there's absolutely no possibility of hooking up with her. Let her really get to know you like I know you. Then maybe when she's over being hurt by the jerk and she's ready to date again, she'll think of you. But don't make that your focus."

"I can't keep my hands off her."

"You not only have to keep your hands off her, you have to stop flirting. No sexual innuendos. Nothing you wouldn't do in front of Jasmine."

Tony wanted to ask Priscilla what was left to talk about. But the front door opened, signaling Jasmine's arrival, and he needed to focus on his daughter.

He went to greet her as she ran inside, arms outstretched. He picked her up in a bear hug and swung her around. This relationship, at least, was in his life for good. And for a couple more years, at least—until Jasmine reached puberty and became a moody teenager—their relationship was entirely good and uncomplicated.

"I missed you a lot, Jazzy."

"I missed you, too, Dad."

He set her down. "Just look at you! You're all tan."

"I spent almost every day at the beach. Where's Samantha?"

"At her dad's for a few days before school starts."

"Oh." Jasmine was clearly disappointed. Ever since Kat and her daughter Samantha had moved in next door, Jas and Samantha had been inseparable. Although Jas was a couple of years older, she adored Samantha and treated her like the little sister she'd never had.

He understood nonblood family ties. The only real family Tony had known as a kid was Ethan and his mom, who'd sort of unofficially adopted him. At least Tony had had a place to crash when things at his own house got ugly.

Tony picked up his daughter's suitcase and followed her down the hall to her room. She would be anxious to put everything away and get settled in. She was a fastidious child, always wanting things neat, clean and organized.

"Want to go for a bike ride?" he asked.

"Ugh, it's too hot."

"We could swim at the rec center." He set her small suitcase on the bed and opened it for her.

"Dad, could you not hover quite so much? I just spent two weeks with Gramma and Grandpa wanting to be with me every second. I need some space."

Tony groaned inwardly. Now he was smothering his own daughter. Was he the only person in the world who didn't need "space"?

"Okay, Sweetie. I'll be out in the yard. After you unwind a little, you can tell me all about your trip."

But out in the yard doing what? It occurred to him that he really had no nonwork interests beyond his backyard. Ethan had his home-improvement projects to keep him busy and now he was talking about buying a boat. Priscilla was always involved in something—recreational shopping, visiting with her friends, charity work, getting a pedicure. And they were both in the thick of paramedic training, which kept them busy.

Tony liked to run and ride his bike, but in the heat of summer he was done with those activities by eight in the morning. When he'd been with Daralee, he'd filled his off days with her. And after their breakup, he'd spent his leisure time mooning over her, plotting to get her back. Then he'd discovered Julie, and his focus had switched to her.

Maybe if he had more varied interests, women like Julie would find him worth something beyond a roll in the hay.

He wandered into the living room, his gaze falling on a bookshelf lined with leather-bound volumes. Priscilla, trying to class his place up a little, had filled Tony's bookcase with more of an eye toward decor than reading pleasure.

Moby Dick. That was an action story, right? They'd even made a movie out of it. He pulled the book off the shelf, found himself a comfortable chair and started to read.

Tony hadn't read a novel since he'd been forced to in high school—and even then he'd relied on Cliff's Notes to pass the test. He found the tiny print and dense prose slow going, but he persevered. If he was going to be friends with Julie, they would have to have something to talk about. Maybe they could talk about books.

That sounded *so* boring. But much as he hated to admit it, he knew Priscilla had a point. He was doing something wrong where women were concerned. He couldn't just keep doing what he'd always done and expect different results.

So, all right, he would be Julie's friend—and he would do it right this time. He would not touch her or flirt with her. He was still hoping to change her mind about the tearoom, but he was beginning to think that was a lost cause. She wouldn't listen to reason and neither would she fall for any emotional pleas. So he would treat her as he did Priscilla, whom he liked and respected. He wouldn't smother her.

In fact, he decided, he'd go even further. If she wanted anything more than friendship from him, ever, she was going to have to make the first move. He was done forever being the seducer, the hunter, the aggressor. He was, from this day forward, Mr. Aloof, Mr. Hard-to-Get. No more handing his heart on a platter to every good-looking woman who batted her eyelashes at him.

If Julie changed her mind, she was going to have to seduce *him*.

THREE DAYS LATER JULIE was ashamed to be standing at the bedroom window at precisely seven o'clock, just when Tony got off his shift. He usually came out the front door of the station and walked to the corner of Willomet, where he turned and headed for his home down the block.

She made sure she was hidden behind the blinds, but it turned out not to matter. This morning he didn't spare her building a glance. He was with Priscilla and Ethan, and the three of them seemed wrapped up in conversation, laughing about something. It was almost as if Tony deliberately avoided looking her way, though that was probably granting herself way too much importance. After the old "just friends" speech, she doubted he was going to think about her much at all.

He'd probably moved on to his next conquest.

Guys like Tony had women standing in line to date him, to sleep with him. He'd probably had his pick of candidates. Why would he waste even a moment's thought on Julie when she'd been so clear with her rejection?

She'd regretted her actions a million ways to Sunday. Though in her mind she knew she'd done the right thing, her heart was arguing with it. Tony was a good guy, as Priscilla had said. How often did one of them come along? Yes, he wanted her, but she wanted him, too, so they were even. Besides, that wasn't the only reason he'd painted over the hurtful graffiti on her back wall or helped her clean up the bar. He liked helping people. Why else would he be a firefighter?

She'd loved Trey—or she thought she had. But what had attracted her to him was his self-assuredness, his clever mind and—if she were being completely, brutally honest—his wealth. Or at least the security his money represented. She'd told herself

Trey was generous. He'd always been taking her out to nice places and surprising her with expensive gifts. She'd told herself he was a hard worker and a good friend.

But looking back, she could see the flaw in her reasoning. It was easy for guys like Trey to be generous. Buying her little baubles was no hardship when his bank account was practically unlimited. But when had he ever been generous with his time?

Would Trey have painted a wall for her? With his own hands? Not likely.

As Tony and his housemates disappeared around the corner, she sighed. She envied them their friendship. After her split with Trey, she'd lost most of her friends, too, even the women. Why would they ally themselves with a penniless, jobless person when they could continue hobnobbing with Trey, riding around in his Porsche, drinking upscale beer and lemon martinis while soaking in his enormous hot tub?

At least she had Belinda. Her little sister was growing up. She had thrown herself wholeheartedly into the tearoom venture with Julie, putting in a lot of hours of drudge work when she wasn't at her waitressing job. Sometimes, she called at odd hours when she had a brainstorm about the decor or the menu or advertising. Yeah, she was still into rock bands and clothes and boys, but Julie sensed a new maturity in Belinda.

She would go far. And Julie and the tearoom

were the keys to helping Belinda reach her potential. Unlike Julie, who had always banged up against the limits of her poor upbringing and her lack of education and training in social graces, Belinda faced no limits. And Julie intended to make sure things stayed that way, no matter what the cost to herself.

Julie forced herself to walk away from the window and start her day. She headed for her tiny shower with its three minutes of hot water, and along with yesterday's grit she washed away her pensive mood. She didn't have time to ponder life's puzzles today. She had walls to paint. She stuck a few pins in her hair to keep it out of her face and out of the paint. Then she headed downstairs, gearing up for the task at hand.

Once she reached the tearoom, she paused a few moments to savor the transformation taking place. The construction had been completed—she'd really only moved one wall so she would have room for a kitchen. And she'd hired a neighborhood guy to paint the tin ceiling, because he'd offered and the price was right. But the walls were all hers.

She spread out her plastic drop cloth, positioned the ladder and opened the first can of the beautiful soft gold paint she'd selected. She thought it would give the place a sort of Tuscan feel.

She'd only covered a few square feet when someone knocked on her front door. She didn't think she had any deliveries scheduled for the day and at first she considered ignoring it, but then she couldn't deny her own curiosity. She climbed down from the ladder, wiped her hands on a rag and padded to the front door, making sure she didn't have any paint on her feet.

Her heart slammed into her chest. Tony. What was he doing here? Even more surprising, he had a little girl with him.

She opened the door. "Hey, how's it going?" he said with a friendly smile, just as if they hadn't parted company on such an awkward note three days earlier.

"It's going fine. And, no, I haven't changed my mind about opening a tearoom." Just in case he'd come over to argue his case again. "I'm painting."

"We know, we saw through the window," the little girl said. "Can we come in and look?"

"Sure. Y'all can tell me if you like the color, although it's too late if you don't. I've bought six nonreturnable gallons of the stuff." She opened the door wider to let them in, but she snagged Tony's arm as he entered. "Are you going to introduce me to your friend?"

The girl giggled.

"This is my daughter, Jasmine."

"Oh." Julie struggled to put the world right side up again. Okay, so Tony had a child. He'd been married before. No big deal. She wasn't antidivorce or anything. It's just that she hadn't thought of him that way. Until this moment he had been, in her mind, the typical bachelor, free and unattached.

But he was a father.

"I guess I never mentioned Jasmine before," he said.

"No, you didn't." Julie found a smile for the adorable young girl. "Hi, Jasmine. I'm Julie."

She was tall and slender—and beautiful, with thick black hair piled carelessly on her head. She looked like Tony around the eyes, but the upturned nose and wide mouth had perhaps come from her mother. She was dressed in baggy blue shorts, a Marine World T-shirt and glittery flip-flops.

"It's nice to meet you, Julie," Jasmine said, polite as can be, extending her hand, which Julie shook. "Do you really own this place?"

"Did you think I made it up?" Tony said.

"Actually, my mother owns it," Julie replied, "but she's an absentee owner. She hasn't been here in years."

Tony looked around. "You planning to paint this whole place by yourself?"

"Do you have any idea what painters charge?" she countered. "It's a big job, but I'm up to it. And Belinda's going to help later."

"We could help, too," Jasmine said. "I know how to paint. I painted my room at home. Purple. It is so cool."

"I appreciate the offer, but you don't have your painting clothes on," Julie pointed out. "If you've painted before, you know how messy it is." She already had dots of gold decorating the old T-shirt she wore.

"We could go home and change," Tony said.

·"That's really nice of you, but… Do you really want to help? I mean, every step I take toward getting the place renovated is another step closer to my opening Belinda's Tearoom—which goes directly against your best interests."

Tony grinned. "Not necessarily. Brady's Tavern could have gold walls."

"Pretty much anything would be an improvement over, well, I'm not sure what to call the current color. Cloudy dirt?"

"More like pukey beige."

Jasmine giggled.

"We'll go change clothes and be right back," Tony said. "Hey, it's that or we'll have to go home and pull weeds."

"Oh, no, not that!" Jasmine said. "I hate weeding. Save me, Julie, please?"

Julie really was in no position to turn down free labor, even if she doubted Tony's motives were completely pure. "Okay. If you really want. I have lots of brushes."

Jasmine clapped her hands together and dragged her father out the door. It was so funny what some children got excited about.

Tony, a dad. That would take some getting used to. The girl had to be nine or ten, at least, which put Tony in his early thirties, probably. She'd thought he was closer to her own age of twenty-five.

By the time the two returned in their old clothes a few minutes later, Julie had prepared an area for Jasmine to work on—a half wall that served to break up the dining room a bit, so it seemed cozier. She gave the girl a wide brush and a coffee can of paint, as well as a bit of instruction.

"I can do this, really," Jasmine said. "I'll be neat, too."

"Knowing her, she won't spill a drop," Tony said so only Julie could hear. "She is the tidiest person in the world."

Julie put Tony to work with a roller, while she started the more detailed brushwork near the wood trim. Both father and daughter worked a while without complaint, seemingly happy. And, true to her word, Jasmine was very neat and very thorough. She didn't cover a lot of territory, but what she did, she did well.

When Julie's path crossed Tony's and her ladder was almost on top of him, she couldn't resist commenting about Jasmine. "I can't believe you didn't tell me you had a daughter."

"It didn't come up," he said. "Anyway, I thought you and I might be…well, you know. And us single dads learn not to blurt out the truth about our kids right out of the gate. Some women don't want to compete with children."

"It wouldn't have bothered me," Julie said. "I like kids."

"Well, anyway, Jasmine's not something I would hide for long. I'm very proud of her. She's the…the shining light in my universe. Sometimes I'm amazed that two ordinary people could have produced such an amazing child."

Seeing the way Tony lit up when he talked about her, Julie softened. Just because Trey wanted to duck his responsibilities as a father didn't mean every man felt the same way. "Does she live with you?"

"I share custody with Natalie, her mom. Our arrangement is pretty loose, especially in the summer. I want to spend time with her now, before she turns into one of those sullen teenagers and I'm not cool enough for her."

"How old is she now?"

He grinned. "Nine going on thirty. I can't keep up with her."

Julie couldn't deny the appeal of this new Tony. Before, he'd been charming in a Casanova sort of way. But now she felt she was seeing more of his true nature. And she had to admit she liked what she saw. And then there was the way his old T-shirt stretched across his shoulders made her want to touch him.

She resisted the urge. Her body hungered for some physical contact with him, even something perfectly innocent. But he'd been giving off definite we're-just-friends-now vibes. She was the one who had told him it wouldn't work, and he'd taken her at her word. It would be wrong for her to suddenly change her mind. Probably foolish, too. She had made her bed, as her mother was fond of saying. Now she could lie in it. Or *not* lie in it with Tony, at any rate.

But, damn, she missed the flirtatious winks, the compliments, the lingering looks.

She shook her head in frustration with herself.

This was what she wanted, wasn't it? She didn't have time for a relationship. She had a tearoom to open and she needed more time to grieve the canceled marriage to Trey.

Why, then, did she feel so sad and empty? So bereaved?

Julie moved to a different spot, closer to Jasmine. "When does school start?" she asked.

"Ugh, next week. Too soon."

"You're going into fourth grade?" Julie guessed.

"Uh-huh."

"I remember fourth grade. That's when stuff gets really interesting. Do you have a favorite subject?"

Jasmine brightened. "Science. And math and creative writing. I have a really good teacher for those classes, Mrs. Jeffries. I think I might want to be a doctor someday. And maybe go to Africa and cure some terrible disease."

"That's very noble," Julie said, impressed that a nine-year-old would think that far ahead. "Makes my wanting to serve people quiche and crepes seem kind of unimportant."

"People have to eat," Jasmine said pragmatically.

Julie laughed. "Yes, they do."

"Anyway, I might become a supermodel instead of a doctor."

Julie smiled. That sounded more like a little girl.

They broke for lunch, and Tony insisted on buying a pizza. Julie insisted just as hard that it should be her treat; they were doing her a huge favor, after all. So they compromised and split the cost.

After lunch, Jasmine seemed a little less enthusiastic about painting.

"I think you guys have done enough," Julie said. "Why don't you go have some fun? Belinda's coming over after her shift at work and she'll help me, so I won't be alone."

"Daddy, you did say something about swimming this afternoon."

"You're right, I did." He checked his watch. "I guess we should go."

"Thanks for letting me paint," Jasmine said to Julie. She was an exceedingly polite child. Someone was raising her right. "When I come here to eat, I'm gonna tell everyone I painted that whole wall all by myself."

"And a beautiful wall it is," Julie said.

"See you around," Tony said. No wink. No sexy grin. Just a wave.

Julie watched them as they crossed the street and disappeared down Willomet Avenue, her heart heavy. Part of her wanted to be included in their intimate circle. But she had to be practical.

Chapter Eight

Belinda arrived just as they left, wearing a baggy pair of overall shorts and a tube top that revealed a little butterfly tattoo on her shoulder. Julie had just about fainted when she'd first spotted it a few weeks ago.

Belinda threw her purse behind the bar. "Was that Tony?"

Julie sighed. "Uh-huh. And his daughter. He's got a daughter."

Belinda's jaw dropped. "Wow. He doesn't seem, you know, dadlike."

"You wouldn't say that if you saw the two of them together."

"Really. What were they doing here? I thought you guys had decided it wasn't going to work out."

"We did. He's just being a good neighbor." And Julie related that morning's events while she set up a painting area for Belinda.

"Now, excuse me, but a guy doesn't spend half a day painting your restaurant—a restaurant he claims he doesn't want you to open—unless he wants something from you. Like sex."

"I dunno, Bel. It didn't seem that way."

"You sound sad."

"I am a little. I shouldn't even be thinking about a new guy right now. But I can't help it. He was cute and sexy before and he really got under my skin. I saw a new side of him today."

"'Cause he has a kid?" Belinda wrinkled her nose. "Doesn't appeal to me at all."

"I didn't think it would me, either." She shrugged again. "Can't explain it. But, I can't help but wonder if I've made a terrible mistake."

A FEW DAYS LATER TONY dropped by again, this time without Jasmine. "Hey, the paint looks great."

"Thanks." It had taken Julie the rest of that first day and all of a second to get it done, but she was pleased with the results. The texturing she'd done had given the walls a sort of antique look. Today she planned to tackle the bar. It was a beautiful thing, solid oak and intricately carved with lions' heads and leaves, but it was scarred and in desperate need of refinishing.

"I'm heading for The Home Depot to get some stuff for the yard," Tony said. "Since you probably go there every day, I thought I'd ask if you needed anything."

Well, how thoughtful. "I really can't think of anything just now. I'm in debt to that store up to my eyeballs anyway. Oh, but there is one little thing you could help with. The bar has a few built-in drawers, and one of them is completely stuck. Maybe you could put a little muscle behind it and yank it out?"

"Sure. Show me."

Was she inventing excuses to keep him around? Yeah, maybe. The drawer really was stuck, but with a hammer she'd probably have been able to get it open on her own. He looked so good in his khaki shorts and soft-blue pocket tee that she had to stick her hands in her pockets to keep them from straying.

She led him behind the bar and pointed to the stubborn drawer.

Tony rubbed his hands together. "Let's see if all the pumping iron pays off." He bent down, grabbed the drawer handle and gave it a mighty yank.

Nothing.

"Guess I have to put some weight behind it." He spread his feet, then gave an even harder pull. The drawer came loose so suddenly it caused Tony to topple backward—right into Julie's legs. Julie grabbed at the edge of the bar and managed to slow her fall, but they both ended up in a heap on the floor. She heard Tony's elbow hit the hardwood planks.

"Are you okay?" Tony immediately asked.

"I'm fine, but how's your elbow?"

As he sat up, he rubbed his arm. "I guess I smacked it pretty good." They both looked at the drawer. It was in pieces. "Julie, I'm sorry. I broke your drawer."

"Never mind about the drawer. I broke your elbow."

"It's fine," he insisted. "I'll have a bruise, that's all."

"Let me get you some ice." She tried to extricate herself and stand up, but he grabbed her hand and tugged her back down to the floor.

"Julie, it's fine."

Oh, he shouldn't have touched her. She felt the warmth and strength of his hand all the way to the pit of her stomach. And he hadn't let her go.

They were only inches apart. Their gazes locked, and she thought for sure he was going to kiss her again. But then he seemed to shake himself out of the sensual spell. He released her hand and looked away. "Maybe ice is a good idea."

Yeah, they should cover their bodies with it. Because nothing else was going to put out the fire.

She touched his face. She couldn't help herself. Wise or not, she wanted him to kiss her. It was hell seeing him and not being able to touch.

"You're making things difficult," he said.

"I don't mean to." And when he still didn't kiss her, she leaned in and kissed him.

Whatever had been making him hesitate vanished. He returned her kiss like a sailor who'd been at sea far too long. As for her, she couldn't hold back or temper her response with restraint. She'd opened Pandora's box.

"I suck at this 'just friends' stuff," she said between fevered kisses.

"Me, too."

In some dim recess of his brain Tony knew this

probably wasn't a smart move. Julie didn't know her mind; she was very likely to reject him again and to regret any kind of intimate contact. But if this was his last chance to convince her they had some amazing chemistry going for them, he wanted to do it right.

He deliberately slowed down the kisses, exploring her mouth in a leisurely way, nibbling her full lower lip. She tasted of something spicy, something exotic he couldn't put a name to.

Although she'd started this, he took full command of it, angling their mouths just right until they fit together, then drinking in the kiss as a man dying of thirst would drink from a well. He slid his fingers into her hair, then one by one found the pins holding it up and slipped them out until the soft strands of golden silk cascaded over his arms.

"You have any deliveries scheduled for today?" he murmured in her ear.

She shivered delicately. "No."

"Any workmen on their way over?"

"Uh-uh."

"Is the door locked?"

"Uh-huh."

He pushed her down onto her back and kissed her some more. "Are you going to tell me to stop?"

She didn't answer for quite some time, choosing instead to kiss his neck. His blood surged hot through his veins.

"No," she finally whispered.

"No what?"

"No, I'm not going to stop you."

"Okay, then." Their fate was sealed. By some miracle, Tony was about to make love to a willing— eager—Julie Polk. He wasn't about to question his good fortune.

He had her paint-spattered T-shirt off in no time. Underneath it she wore an ivory-colored silky wisp of a bra that left little to his imagination, but off it came, as well. Her breasts were creamy and so flawless he was almost afraid to touch them. When he did, Julie closed her eyes and gave a trembling sigh.

"Too many clothes," Julie said.

"I can fix that." Shorts, shirt, shoes, socks, underwear, everything was gone in seconds flat. When Julie looked amused by his rapid-fire striptease, he added, "Firefighters have to learn to dress and undress quickly." He smiled, then cupped her chin in his hand and kissed her again, more aggressively this time. She would never mistake his desire for her as passing for lukewarm.

He considered moving somewhere more comfortable than a hard floor, but then decided that he didn't care if she didn't. Besides, relocating might cause one of them to come to their senses, and he didn't want to risk that. He'd have made love to Julie on the back of a camel, if that was what was the only available option.

He unzipped her shorts and pulled them down her legs. He could undress a woman pretty quickly, too. He paused only briefly to admire how she looked in silky bikini panties that barely covered anything, then they too joined the pile of discarded clothing.

Suddenly, she stiffened and pulled back. "Oh, no."

"What?" Tony thought he would die if she changed her mind now.

"I don't have any birth control." She sounded both relieved and miserable.

"Got it covered—uh, no pun intended." Thank God. For ten years he'd never gone anywhere without protection, whether he thought he would need it or not—not after he'd unintentionally gotten Natalie pregnant.

He honestly hadn't come here with seduction in mind. He'd been holding fast to Priscilla's advice to treat Julie as a friend. But he sure was glad he'd been prepared for anything.

He pulled her on top of him to save her the bite of the wood floor, then reveled in every inch of her bare skin as it touched his. He wanted to feel her everywhere at once. He ran one hand across a smooth flank, then gently cupped one breast, testing its weight, letting the hard nipple scrape across his palm.

His arousal stirred with eagerness.

Julie couldn't believe this was happening. She'd had a lot of mixed feelings about Tony and had wondered if she could change her mind, but she had never imagined they would suddenly come together on the floor behind her bar. She might as well have been tied to railroad tracks, for all the ability she had to halt the inevitable outcome.

As if she really wanted to.

Tony maneuvered so deftly she never even realized it until she felt the press of his arousal against her. He'd already taken care of protecting her—when had he done that? She couldn't remember. But he didn't enter her right away. Instead, he smoothed her hair away from her face and looked deeply into her eyes.

"You know I'm crazy about you, right?"

"Um…" At this point, did it matter?

"I am. I don't just go around making love because I have the chance to. It means something to me. It's important that you know that."

"Uh-huh." Sorry, she was no longer verbal. Her brain was preoccupied with other, more important things. Like processing the ten million sensations coming from below her waist. But she stored his words away for later examination.

"I won't hurt you, will I?"

She was going to hurt *him* if he didn't enter her in the next ten seconds. But all she could do was shake her head. What, did he think that she might be a virgin?

She poised herself over him, her invitation impossible to misunderstand.

Tony grinned. "All right, then." But he didn't rush. He pulled her down on top of him slowly, inch by inch, allowing her to appreciate each new sensation as it came.

He filled her completely, stretched her until she was sure she couldn't accommodate any more, then pushed again.

Oh, she'd had no idea, no idea at all it could feel like this. To her utter surprise, she reached a climax before he'd even started to move. She writhed ecstatically on top of him, trying to keep her cries to a minimum because she was actually shocked by the strength of her response to him.

"Let it loose, Julie," he said. "There's no one here but us." But then his grin faded as his rational side lost control of the situation and his body took over. He thrust into her over and over, rocking them back and forth and side to side and every which way. Her foot caught a broom and sent it toppling with a crash just as Tony reached his own crescendo.

After a few moments of gasping for breath, he laughed. She laughed, too, a lovely release of tension. Weren't they a pair? She sagged against him, her fingers tangled in his hair as their breathing slowed.

"That was one for the record books," he said. "I've heard sex compared to falling off the edge of the world before, but for a minute there I thought I really did."

"I guess we could have gone upstairs first," she said, feeling the first tendrils of embarrassment at the way she'd just acted—like a cat in heat. "But it wouldn't have been much better. I put all my money into the tearoom and I couldn't afford the luxury of a bed."

"A bed is a necessity, babe, not a luxury."

"I'm starting to see why."

He stroked her back, sending aftershock chills through her body.

"So really," she asked drowsily, "how come you just happened to have a condom in your pocket?"

"Be Prepared—that's my motto."

"You were never a Boy Scout."

"How do you know that?"

"Because you were too busy feeling up Girl Scouts to work on merit badges. And besides, they don't give out merit badges for seduction."

He laughed. "You think you've got my number, but you might be surprised. Were you a Girl Scout?"

"Campfire Girl." For all of a couple of weeks, until her mother found out she would have to pay for a uniform. "I need a shower."

"Want some company?"

"No! I... I mean, this is weird. I need time to think about it."

Tony sighed. "I wish women wouldn't think so much."

"Someone has to or we'd still be living in caves. Maybe men are credited with most of the great inventions and advances in society, but only because women told them what to go out and invent."

Tony laughed again, but he did let her go. She rolled to the side and sat up. "I'll be right back, okay?" She pulled on her T-shirt, underwear and shorts—she couldn't wander about naked in the tearoom, not when someone could look in if they had a mind to—and retired to the ladies' room to freshen up. She heard the door down the hall close and knew Tony was doing the same in the other washroom.

She felt more relaxed than she had in a long time.

She washed her hands with vanilla-scented soap, which filled the whole bathroom with a wonderful fragrance. When she was done, she emerged to find Tony leaning against the bar, fully dressed. Her wonderful mood immediately evaporated when she saw the look on Tony's face.

"Julie, there's something I have to tell you."

"What?" she asked warily.

"The, um, condom broke."

"What?" She closed her eyes, then opened them again, panic rising in her chest. This could not be happening. They'd been careful. They'd been responsible. "How did that happen?"

"I'm not really qualified to explain latex failure."

"How can you joke about this? It isn't funny. It's horrible! An unplanned pregnancy is just what I need right now."

"I'm sorry. It's not on my agenda either."

"Well…well, what do we do?"

"I don't know that there's anything to do right now."

Her head started to spin, but there was nowhere to sit down. She put a hand on the freshly painted wall to steady herself. "So we just have to wait to see if I'm pregnant?"

"I'm sorry," he said again, which didn't help. Logically, she knew it wasn't Tony's fault, but she was angry, and he was the closest target.

She sank to the floor and put her head in her hands.

Tony was beside her in an instant. "Hey, look at me."

She couldn't. She was horrified. She'd never

done anything else this crazy and irresponsible in her whole life.

He lifted her chin up and forced her to look at him. "It'll be okay."

"Easy for you to say. You're not the one who's probably pregnant as we speak." She lowered her head into her hands. He wasn't the one whose life would be irrevocably changed if she had a child out of wedlock. She visualized herself working in the tearoom, seating her customers and refilling iced-tea glasses, her stomach looking like a beach ball and no husband in sight.

Wouldn't that impress her high-society clientele?

Meanwhile, he would be off in macho land, on to his next conquest, maybe *engaged*. No, that wasn't fair to color every man with the same brush. Just because Trey had tried to weasel out of his paternal responsibilities didn't mean Tony would do the same thing.

Really, she had no idea what Tony would do if faced with an unexpected child. She didn't know him that well. He *seemed* like a good guy, a good dad to Jasmine. But Julie surely couldn't rely on her own judgment when it came to men. Trey had seemed like a good guy, too.

"You do want kids someday, right?" he asked.

Julie sensed her answer was important to him, so she made it as honest as she could. "Sure, of course. But not now! Anyway, that's not why I'm upset. I'm upset because I did something stupid. I should know better. What a horrible example I'm setting for my sister!" She pressed a hand to her abdomen and willed her panic to go away. Panic wouldn't help anything.

"Do you share everything with Belinda?"

"No, but if I'm pregnant, I won't have to share."

"The chance of that is small."

"Not that small." She sighed. "If I bring a child into the world, I want it to have the benefit of two parents. Two married, committed parents."

Then she remembered that Tony's daughter didn't have that and she backpedaled a bit. "I'm not criticizing the fact you're a single dad, believe me. I'm sure you must have tried to make things work, and it seems like you're doing a great job with Jasmine. Still, to even risk having a child when I'm not in any position to be a good parent—that is just the height of irresponsibility. I broke up with Trey because he did that."

"You know," Tony said carefully, "if you just love your kids, it makes up for an awful lot. Working eighty-hour weeks to provide them with stuff doesn't hold a candle to loving them. Ethan grew up with only one parent. His mom didn't have much money, but she raised him right. They're still really close."

So Tony thought she would do fine as a single mother? *Thanks for the vote of confidence.* But it wasn't exactly the response she would have preferred.

Maybe he was right about one thing, however. One committed parent was probably better than two who didn't care as much. Her parents had gotten married "because they had to." They'd taken responsibility for Julie, but they hadn't been the most devoted mother and father.

Quality, not quantity, was the important thing.

Tony was gazing out into space, lost in thought. He'd mentioned Ethan's mother but not his own. Had he felt loved as a child?

"Tony, I think this was a mistake."

Her words made him flinch, and she immediately wished she had couched her feelings in softer terms.

"We can't take it back," he said.

"No. But we should have a little more sense."

"Aw, you aren't going to give me the 'just friends' speech again, are you? I don't think I could stand that."

Finally, she found a smile. "I guess that doesn't work very well for us, does it? But you can't expect... I'm not ready to... I have to give a hundred percent to the tearoom right now."

"You couldn't even spare one percent for me?"

"Would you really want that?"

"No. I'd like to be the most important thing in your life. I'd like for you to worship the ground I walk on. But given the likelihood of that at this point in your life, I'll take what I can get. At least until you get your life put back together."

She pinched the bridge of her nose. "It's a mess, isn't it?"

"Everyone's life gets messy at some point. But, Julie, I have to ask you something. Do you see any future in it? In us? I'm not saying we should get all serious right away, I'm not saying that at all. But I don't want to be your recreational sex buddy, your boy toy, your gigolo. So if you're saying to yourself, 'Tony's fun, but I could never take him seriously,' or 'Tony's okay till someone better comes along,' tell me now."

She looked at him a long time before answering. "Some woman did a real number on you."

"Not any particular woman," he said. "It's more like a syndrome. Women don't take me seriously."

"For the record, Tony, I'm not thinking any of those things. Right now it's hard to think about the future, at least not anything beyond paying next month's bills. But I don't see you as a diversion. I like you a lot. I want the chance to get to know you better. I certainly wouldn't rule out the possibility that we could be, well, you know…long-term. Someday. Who knows?"

Tony grinned. "That's all I need to hear."

Maybe not all. "I know I'm a little flaky right now. But you can count on one thing from me—I'll be honest. I despise game-playing of any kind. But I want the same from you. If we can just tell each other the truth, maybe this can work out."

He nodded agreement. "Yeah. Absolutely." But it seemed to her that his gaze got just a bit evasive.

Chapter Nine

Tony left because Julie virtually kicked him out, claiming she had work to do and she couldn't do it if he was around distracting her. But she'd given him hope. She'd agreed that they could be together, at least sometimes. Though he would never be content with just crumbs of her affection, he realized that for now that was all she had to offer and he was willing to live with it. For a while.

There was just one teensy fly in the ointment. It was that little speech she'd given about honesty and game-playing.

How would she feel if she knew that the reason he'd approached her in the first place, the reason he'd flirted and pretended to want to help her, was so he could manipulate himself into a position of influence in her life and convince her to reopen Brady's Tavern?

What if she found out? He was in for some merciless razzing from his fellow firefighters when they discovered he and Julie had hit it off. Most of them would only wish him luck, but not all of them. Some were still angry and spiteful that Julie had destroyed Brady's Tavern. Any one of them could let it slip, accidentally or on purpose, that Tony's interest in Julie hadn't originated from the purest of motives.

He should tell her himself, that's what he should do. Maybe she would think it was funny—that he'd set out to seduce her so he could convince her to preserve his bar and had ended up falling for her instead.

Yeah, right. Or maybe she wouldn't think it was so funny.

He would tell her anyway, he decided. So long as that secret remained between them, he wouldn't be able to rest. But he wouldn't tell her yet. Their relationship was too new, too fragile. He would give it a couple of weeks.

He planted some fall flowers in the bed in front of his house, then took Dino for a long walk. Now that the worst of the summer heat had passed, walks were a pleasure again. He let the pup's unbridled affection soothe him. Dogs weren't hard to figure out. Feed them, walk them, pet them, and they'd love you for life. Just like him.

A woman was a bit more complicated, and Julie seemed to be the most complicated of all.

Jasmine arrived that evening, weighed down by a half-dozen shopping bags in different colors. Oh, boy, a little shopaholic in the making.

"Daddy!" She dropped the bags and ran to hug him with all the delicacy of a freight train, and he stumbled backward as they threw their arms around each other.

"Hi, Jazzy. Looks like you bought out the stores."

"Mom took me school shopping today."

"Did you use my card?" Natalie had a VISA she used only for Jasmine-related expenses, and Tony paid the bill.

"Yeah, but we found some good bargains. Did you plant new flowers out front? They look good."

"Yeah, I did. Thanks. Nice change of subject, too." Tony was actually pleased she'd noticed. He'd become a complete yard nut since moving in here. Before, he'd always lived in apartments and hadn't given green things a single thought. But since Priscilla had provided him with any sort of outdoor tool he wanted, so long as he took care of the yard, he'd discovered a new calling.

"Have you seen Julie again?" she asked, the question laced with innuendo. Now how had she figured that out?

"I might have."

"She's soooo much nicer than Daralee," Jasmine said.

He put his arm around her as they walked toward the kitchen. "You didn't like Daralee? I thought she was pretty nice to you. She bought you a ring, didn't she?"

"'Cause she was trying to impress *you*. She didn't like me at all. If you'd married her, she'd have sent me off to boarding school. I couldn't stand her."

That gave Tony pause. "What about my other girlfriends? Did you hate them, too?"

"Some of them."

He'd never considered how his social life affected his daughter. She'd always been very accepting of whomever he happened to be dating, never jealous or resentful. At least not that she showed him.

"From now on, I want you to tell me if you don't like some girl I'm dating, okay? I need to know these things."

"I like Julie. She's nice—and pretty. Then again, all your girlfriends are pretty."

"You say it like I have a harem or something."

"Also, Julie didn't treat me like a baby."

"I like her, too, kiddo. So what's the homework situation?"

"Done."

"Then you can show me your new clothes. How about that?"

"Okay. Mom said not to show you the price tags. But Daddy, I'm in fourth grade now. How I look is *really* important."

"How you act is more important, Jas." But he didn't feel like giving her a lecture now. "Come on, show me your new duds. I won't look at the price tags."

Tony sat on his daughter's bed, and Jasmine went into the closet to change into her various new outfits, emerging like a model on the runway, gliding across the room with her nose in the air and pirouetting for his inspection.

"Very nice," he said of her latest offering. "The skirt's pretty short."

"Daaaaaddy."

"Get used to it. You'll be hearing it a lot over the next few years. Okay, what else?"

"That's all," she said hastily.

"What's in that bag?" He pointed to a shiny pink bag that Jasmine had kicked off to the side.

"Uh, nothing, Dad. Just underwear and socks and stuff."

He looked more closely at the bag. "From Paris Intimates?"

"I got a bra, okay?" she blurted out.

Tony sat up straight. Had he heard right? "You're only nine years old!" Girls in his family did tend to mature early, but still.

"Almost ten, and I need it! It's really embarrassing!" She burst into tears and stormed out of the room. Moments later he heard the bathroom door slam.

Tony put Jasmine's pillow over his head and groaned. This could not be happening. He would have to spend the rest of his life *not* looking in the vicinity of his daughter's chest, because he didn't want to know whether it was true or not.

A FEW DAYS LATER AT the fire station, Tony had just cooked some french fries and dumped them onto paper towels when Otis strolled into the kitchen. "Smells good. At least you rookies are good for something."

"I don't see how you can smell anything but Ben-Gay, the way you slather that stuff on your old, creaking joints."

Otis narrowed his eyes, then laughed. "Touché. I hate it when rookies can't give as good as they get." He snagged a hot fry, tossing it back and forth between his hands to cool it. "So how are things going with juicy Julie?" He accompanied the question with a leer.

"Okay," Tony said, offering up as little detail as possible. In truth, things were better than okay. Over the past few days he'd been pitching in at the tearoom, helping Julie with various projects, and she'd let him. Though he'd have preferred to take her out to dinner—or even just walk to the park and feed the ducks—at least they were talking, getting to know each other better. Julie had seemed more relaxed and twice more they'd made love—on her lumpy sofa. Not as good as a bed but better than the floor. She had not mentioned the possible pregnancy again, but he knew it was on her mind.

It was on his mind, too.

"You get her into bed yet?" Otis asked.

Tony's whole face tightened. "That topic is not up for discussion."

"So you haven't," Otis said smugly. He put some water on to boil for tea, giving himself an excuse to hang around.

Tony practically bit through his tongue. Otis was deliberately maligning Tony's manhood to get a rise out of him, but he would not give up any details.

"I don't know how you expect to convince that gal to give up her tearoom if you can't even get her into bed."

Tony wasn't normally prone to violence. He'd always been known as the one with the cool head, the prototypical "I'm a lover, not a fighter" kind of guy. But he really wanted to punch Otis. His right hand clenched into a fist.

That was as far as it went, however. If he got involved in a fistfight with a senior firefighter—with anyone, really—while on duty, he'd be in the unemployment line faster than a bullet train. During the first year, rookies could be let go for almost any reason.

If he wanted to defend Julie's honor, he had to do it with words.

"You're still trying to bring Brady's back, right?"

He sighed. "It seems pretty hopeless."

"So you're giving up. Man, I knew we shouldn't have sent a boy to do a man's job."

Tony's blood was slowly coming to a simmer, but he sensed a full boil was on the way. "You're welcome to try."

"Not me. I'm not her type. But maybe Carl Dutton. You know him?"

Tony was afraid he did. He was the guy who'd patched up Julie's hand when she'd cut it on the glass and he'd spent far too much time caressing her hand and arm, in Tony's opinion.

"Dutton's been talking about what a hottie Julie is ever since he fixed up her hand. Think maybe I'll tell him the field's wide-open, you've struck out."

Tony turned on Otis, pointing his spatula at him. "You tell Dutton to keep away from Julie. She doesn't need some stud sniffing around her door. She has enough on her plate."

Otis just laughed. "Veracruz, can't you tell when I'm jerking your chain? You got such a bad case for that girl it might as well be tattooed to your forehead. I warned you not to fall in love."

"Otis!"

Both men turned to see Priscilla standing in the doorway.

"Leave Tony alone. Anyway, he's not in love. He hasn't known Julie long enough to be in love. I've been trying to hammer that fact home to him, and you're going to ruin everything."

Otis smiled sheepishly. "Just havin' a bit of fun."

"And get your paws off those french fries or they'll all be gone before the dinner bell rings."

"Yes, Ma'am. Sometimes you sound just like my ex-wife."

"Which one?" Priscilla quipped as Otis set a pitcher of tea on the table.

Otis sauntered out, and Priscilla went to work slicing tomatoes for hamburgers. "You shouldn't let him get to you like that. You know he's just trying to get a rise out of you."

"I know. I don't mind him razzing me so much, but when he talks dirt about Julie, it gets to me."

Priscilla sighed. "There's something you should know. Some of the guys are getting together and pooling their money. They're talking about forming a partnership so they can buy Julie out."

"Really?" The thought was intriguing. If Julie

didn't have that damn tearoom to renovate and open and run, maybe she would have more time for him. He immediately recognized the selfishness contained in that thought, but there it was.

"You're in favor of the idea?" Priscilla asked, surprised.

"I think Julie's tearoom is destined for failure. As much as I'd like to see Brady's reopened, I also don't want her hurt. If she sold out now, she might come out better in the end." But he was pretty sure she wouldn't see it that way.

"There's more to the story. If she doesn't sell, they're talking about buying out her lien holders, then foreclosing if she misses any payments."

Tony winced. "Can they do that?"

"I don't know anything about property law, but Jim Peterson's wife is a real-estate broker, and she said it all depends on how the loans are structured. But it's a possibility."

"Julie could lose everything." That wasn't what he wanted, but he didn't think there was any way in the world she would listen to his advice regarding her property.

Later in the day, Tony talked to Jim Peterson. It was all true—the partnership papers were actually being drawn up. They called themselves the Brady's Consortium. "You don't like the idea?" Peterson asked.

Hell. He'd never felt so torn in his life. If he stuck up for Julie, he'd be seen as a traitor—and he already had enough problems being accepted on equal terms here at the station. But he couldn't honestly say he was in favor of putting pressure tactics on Julie. She was so determined to move forward with her plans. So determined that she wouldn't listen to reason.

"I like Julie," he confessed. "I can't help it. I don't want to see her hurt."

"Look at it this way," Peterson said. "If we let her alone, she'll fail on her own. Then she'll *want* to sell. But I guarantee she won't get as good an offer."

ABOUT A WEEK LATER THE partnership was a reality. Peterson, Otis, Bing Tate and a couple of guys from other stations and other shifts had put it together. They had an offer for Julie—and they wanted Tony to present it to her.

"Since I'm not part of the partnership, I'm not sure I'm the ideal candidate to talk to her," Tony said.

"She's let you in closer than anyone else," Otis pointed out. "She won't let any of the rest of us through the front door. C'mon, do it for Brady's."

"I'll try." But he didn't think he would get very far.

The next day he walked over to the tearoom with papers in hand. Who knew? Maybe Julie would welcome the offer. It seemed fair to him.

She greeted him with a big smile, and his heart lurched as it always did at the sight of her. But she had shadows under her eyes and she looked as if she might have lost weight. She was working too hard.

He let her show him her latest project—a mosaic

countertop made with broken china in the ladies' room. It was a real work of art. "You did that yourself?"

"Uh-huh."

"That's amazing." He had to admit he was impressed with the way things were coming along. All of the woodwork and the floor gleamed with new stain. She had tables and chairs now. Some of the walls had artwork on them. The curtains she'd been sewing, night after night, were finished and ready to hang.

"Listen, Julie, do you have a minute to talk about something serious? I have a business proposition."

"Huh?"

"Just... Let's sit down." They sat at one of the tables, and Tony explained the offer as clearly and succinctly as he could. Her face showed nothing. She was listening, but her expression was carefully blank.

"It's a good offer," he said. "The guys aren't trying to rip you off. You're in the best position right now—before you open. If you should decide to sell later, and let's say the tearoom isn't performing as you hope, the offer will go down." And then he explained about the contingency plan to buy out her lien holders. She needed to know all of it. "I also want you to know that I'm not part of this partnership. I have nothing to gain from this."

She folded her arms and glared at him. "Except to get your bar back."

"That's totally secondary at this point. I don't want to see you get hurt. I think accepting this offer would be the best route for you to take. You'd come out with some significant cash and you could start again somewhere else."

"Start again?" She looked at him as if he was crazy. "After all the work I've put into this? Let me ask you something, Tony. How do you feel about being a firefighter?"

He was thrown off by her question and had no idea where she was going, but he couldn't think of anything to do but answer honestly. "I love it. I love everything about it. I'm just a rookie, but I know this is what I want to do till I'm old and gray."

"And does it occur to you that I might have dreams, too?"

"Well, sure. Everybody's entitled to dream."

"Until recently, I had a career I loved. I was an up-and-coming manager at Bailey-Davidson's and I ran the tearoom there. I loved it. I loved everything about it—the food, the customers, the beautiful chandeliers, the soft music." She got a dreamy expression as she talked about her work.

He knew the basic facts of her previous employment. Her former fiancé and his family hadn't exactly fired her, but she'd been made to feel very uncomfortable and so she'd quit.

"I really didn't know what I was going to do after I left," she continued. "I'd worked at Bailey-Davidson's since I was sixteen. But then Uncle Brady died, and I got this wonderful new opportunity to open my own tearoom.

"Belinda's Tearoom is *my* dream. Owning a

grungy bar is not. Having a pile of cash is not. Sure, I have a brilliant sister to put through college and parents who are depending on this so they can retire with dignity. But I want this for myself, too."

She picked up the papers he'd laid out and shoved them back at him. "You can tell your pals where to stick this offer. I'm not selling."

Well, that hadn't gone well. But had he really expected anything different? Strangely he found himself smiling. He was *glad* she'd refused the offer. And for the first time, he was starting to believe she could make the tearoom a success. Anyone who was that passionate about a dream had an advantage over those just seeking a profit.

"Good," he said. "I hope Belinda's turns out to be the best damn tearoom on the planet."

She stared at him, puzzled, as if she didn't know quite what to make of his sudden about-face.

"I need to get back home," he said. "Jas and I have plans. You want to join us later?"

"I can't," she said. He was getting used to her refusals, though he still had to force himself not to try to cajole her into putting aside her work to have fun. She got cranky when he did.

As he was heading out the door, she called his name.

"Yeah?"

"I'm not pregnant," she blurted out. "So you don't have to worry about that anymore."

He let the news sink in, expecting to feel a rush of relief. But, strangely, he felt a bit let down.

"Hmm. As I recall, you were the one worrying, not me." No, he didn't want another unplanned child. But the thought of having a child with Julie—it wasn't really that scary. He wasn't sixteen anymore.

"YOU SHOULD TELL HER the truth," Priscilla pronounced during their next shift. They'd gotten stuck with bathroom duty again. It was particularly unrewarding working with Priscilla because she was the world's worst bathroom scrubber. It wasn't that she didn't try. She seemed to put a lot of energy into it. But her efforts were ineffectual. Tony always ended up remopping any floor she'd tried to clean.

Now he had the double pleasure of redoing her work and getting a lecture, too. He probably should have kept his mouth shut, but he'd wanted a woman's perspective on how Julie might react to knowing he'd never married Jasmine's mother.

"Lots of people have babies in their teens," Priscilla continued. "It's not like you did it on purpose. And you're a wonderful father to Jasmine."

"Thanks, but I suspect Julie won't see it that way. I didn't marry Natalie."

"But you would have. You were willing to, right?"

"Of course. It seemed like the only thing to do. But her parents discouraged that. And it was a good thing. We'd never have made it as a married couple. Heck, we'd broken up before we even found out she was pregnant." And he knew it was a lot of strain on a relationship, having a baby. He couldn't understand how any marriage survived it.

Priscilla was quiet for a few moments, leaning against her mop, staring out into space. Her sudden change of mood made him wonder what he'd said wrong. But then she shook herself out of it and returned to her mopping with renewed vigor, spreading dirty water around in circles and ruining everything he'd just cleaned. "But you've stayed on good terms and you've always put Jasmine first. I think Julie would admire that."

"Not given her history."

"What's her history, exactly? All I know is she broke up with a guy not long ago."

"Her fiancée got his housekeeper pregnant and then had the poor girl deported before she could give birth. Julie only found out two weeks before—"

Priscilla gasped.

"What?"

"Trey Davidson. I'd heard some rumors, but I didn't think they were true. He said his fiancée went psycho on him and that's why the wedding was called off. Is he the one?"

Tony tried to figure a way out of this. He wasn't supposed to spread the story around—Julie had made him promise not to.

"Don't worry," Pris said before he could confirm or deny. "I won't say anything to anyone. That's awful!"

"Not only did she lose her fiancé, but she lost her job and her town house."

"It's amazing she bounced back the way she has.

And it's amazing she would get anywhere near another guy so soon. That says something about your powers of persuasion."

Tony finished cleaning the last toilet. He took the mop out of her hands so she wouldn't mess up anything else. "Just for that, I'm going to finish your mopping for you." Or they'd never get out of that bathroom.

"Thanks. I'll go check on dinner."

She was even worse at cooking than she was at mopping. But he let her go. He'd been hoping Priscilla would encourage him not to tell, but no, she had to go and push him to be honest.

Things were going so well between Tony and Julie. Yesterday, Julie had actually decided to take a few hours off from her feverish preparations for tomorrow's grand opening. She'd called Tony, and they'd gone to Kidd Springs Park and had a picnic lunch, then played Frisbee with Dino. Later, they'd gone back to his place and made love—on an actual bed. They'd foraged in his kitchen for dinner, feasting on a strange array of leftover pizza, meat loaf and fresh pears. They'd talked about all kinds of things— even *Moby Dick* and *Ivanhoe,* his current reading project.

She'd stayed the whole night, and Tony had imagined how it could be like that every day. He could definitely get used to it.

If he told Julie all his dirty little secrets, it could end in a heartbeat.

He couldn't do it. Not yet.

Chapter Ten

At five in the morning, Julie opened her eyes and sat bolt upright, her heart pounding. She'd had a nightmare that a pipe had burst and flooded the tearoom.

She'd never been prone to prophetic dreams, but just in case, she raced downstairs in her pajamas to check. All was dark and quiet and everything looked fine.

Her chef, André, would already be at the farmers' market downtown, selecting meat, fish and produce. Lisa, her pastry chef, would be hard at work on a selection of desserts. And somehow it was all going to come together for her first day as a restaurateur.

It had to.

Many people had said it was impossible, but she was so close to running out of money that she needed to get Belinda's open and pulling in cash as quickly as possible. She had sold everything she owned just to get this far—including the baubles

Trey had given her. She had balloon payments to make to her lien holders in a few weeks, and André had demanded a month's salary in advance.

But despite all the setbacks and naysayers, today it was going to happen. She'd installed a professional kitchen in record time, had gotten city permits and even transferred Brady's liquor license so she could sell wine. She'd hired her staff and hung the sign. She'd put up her beautiful curtains, arrayed her brass coffee urns on the bar, arranged the dishes, linens and flatware.

She'd sent out invitations to the highest-income zip codes in Dallas, offering a free dessert to anyone who came in for lunch.

She suspected her first day would be hectic and have its ups and downs. But she knew this business well. She knew what ladies who lunched would like. She'd seen to every detail.

Julie showered and dressed with care in one of her favorite outfits—a designer skirt and silk blouse she'd bought at Bailey-Davidson's a few months ago. Even with her employee discount, the price had been outrageous. But it fit so well and made her feel confident, so it was the perfect choice for today.

As soon as she returned downstairs, her pastry chef arrived with a carload of beautiful cakes, pies and cookies. André, along with his two assistants, was busy preparing the soups and quiches and taking care of all the prep work.

Julie stood in her kitchen and watched her employees moving around the room as if they'd worked there for years. André barked out orders from time to time, and his crew scurried to do his bidding, but he was entitled to be a bit high-strung on this first day.

She double-checked the day's specials—mushroom-and-artichoke quiche, tomato-basil soup and carrot cake—and wrote them up on her chalkboard menu.

It really was happening!

She had made sure that Trey and his parents had received invitations. Would they connect Belinda's Tearoom with Julie Polk? Or would her invitation go right into the wastebasket without a second thought? She fantasized about the Davidsons showing up for the grand opening, unexpectedly encountering Julie or Belinda.

Wouldn't they be surprised?

Julie would be perfectly gracious, of course, acting as if nothing was wrong. Or even as if they were strangers—as if she'd already forgotten them.

She had another fantasy, too, that Tony would come for lunch today. Dressed in a suit, his unruly hair trimmed for the occasion, he would take her hands and exclaim, "You've worked a miracle. I never should have tried to talk you out of opening a tearoom."

Although he'd refrained from saying anything discouraging this past week, she hadn't forgotten his earlier predictions. She wanted to prove him wrong. She wanted to prove everybody wrong.

Tony had made some good points about the challenges Belinda's faced. But she couldn't help the yearning inside her—not just to have a business that made a profit but to have security and respect. To accomplish something, to make her mark.

As opening time drew near, the butterflies went crazy in her stomach. She checked with the kitchen every five minutes to be sure everything was on schedule, until finally André chased her away with a spatula and told her to stay out.

Everything was going too smoothly. It made her suspicious. Nothing was ever this easy for her—nothing.

Then the phone rang. It was one of her newly hired waitresses. "My car won't start," she wailed. "Now I have to wait for the auto club. As soon as they get here, I'll have them drop me at a bus stop, but I'm still going to be at least an hour late. Today of all days!"

Julie understood such things. "It's okay, Sara," she said calmly. "Just get here when you can." She'd scheduled five wait staff, including Belinda, so one person being late wasn't a catastrophe.

Then Tommy, one of her waiters, called in sick. She'd known things were going too smoothly.

As she was pondering whether to drag one of the chef's assistants out of the kitchen and train him to wait tables, someone pounded on her front door.

An early customer? Surely not. She peeked out the window and saw a Hispanic woman with a baby standing there. The woman looked vaguely familiar, but Julie couldn't place her. She opened the door. "Yes?"

"I'm Eloisa." At Julie's blank look, she continued. "Eloisa Tinajero. I worked at dollar store." And she pointed down the street.

Julie finally recognized the woman as the sweet but insecure clerk from Dollar Olé on the next block, which had gone out of business the week before. She always *tried* to help, but she was hampered by the fact that her English wasn't too good.

"I need job," the woman blurted out rather desperately. "I cook, wait tables, wash dishes—anything. Dollar Olé close. I can't pay my rent."

The poor woman was almost in tears. How and why had she sought out Julie, and on this day of all days? "Come on in," she said. She would at least give the woman a hot cup of coffee.

"You give me job?" she asked hopefully.

Julie thought about it. She was short a waitress. But she needed servers who were experienced and polished—and who could speak flawless English. Still, Eloisa was neat and well groomed. She could at least refill water glasses and clear tables.

"All right. We'll try you out as a...an assistant waitress."

"Oh, thank you. You teach me menu, I can remember."

"What about the baby?"

"Josephina? She can stay with me. She good baby, never cry."

"No, no, she can't stay here. You'll have to find—"

But Eloisa didn't let her finish. She threw her

arms around Julie's neck. "Thank you so much. I work hard, you see."

Julie just closed her eyes. This was surreal. But the craziness was only beginning.

Eloisa made up a pallet for the baby in Julie's office. She nursed the baby and then put her down for a nap, and Josephina went right to sleep. Julie crossed her fingers that the infant's angelic behavior would continue.

Then she didn't have any more time to worry, because the rest of her wait staff was arriving. She gave them their assignments, then asked Annette, whose Spanish was good, to take Eloisa under her wing.

At ten to eleven everything was in place. The bakery case was filled with mouthwatering cakes and pies, cookies, brownies and dessert bars. The brewing coffee provided a subtle background scent. The piped-in music was a concerto.

There was no trace anywhere of that old stale-beer-and-cigarettes stench that had once permeated the place. Everything was clean, stylish, downright beautiful.

Belinda came to stand beside Julie and took her hand. "You really did it. It's an amazing place. I still can't believe you named it after me."

"It's for your future, after all. Let's rip the paper off the windows!"

They did, and in the matter of a few seconds, daylight was pouring in through the sparkling glass. Now it looked like a real restaurant. All they needed was customers.

"Let's go see if anyone's pulled into the parking lot yet," Belinda said. In her eagerness, she made Julie think of Christmas morning.

As they walked through the storeroom, one of the kitchen staff, Marc, came in to grab something from a shelf. He and Belinda collided, then stopped and stared at each other for a heart-stopping few seconds.

"Oh, hi, Marc."

"Belinda. You coming to hear us play tonight?"

"If you can get me in," Belinda said dreamily.

Oh, for heaven's sake. "Belinda," Julie warned once Marc had gone, "you're not going to clubs, are you? You're not legal drinking age yet."

"I don't drink," she said. "I go for the music." She lowered her voice. "And Marc is so gorgeous. I'm glad you hired him."

If Julie had realized Belinda had the hots for Marc, she would have vetoed André's decision to take him on. But she didn't have time to worry about that now. She grabbed her sister's arm. "Come on. We'll talk later."

Belinda seemed to shake herself from a daze. They peeked out the back dōor. The first car had arrived, a red Mercedes that Julie recognized.

"Uh-oh," she murmured.

"Trouble?"

Julie's stomach tensed. "Megan Von Snell, a former boss from Bailey-Davidson's."

Belinda frowned. "You don't think Trey sent spies to sabotage our grand opening, do you?"

What a horrible thought! "We'll see." They watched covertly as Megan, who'd arrived alone, followed the flower-lined stone path to the front door. Her face was hard to read.

Julie and Belinda quickly retreated through the kitchen and headed back into the dining room in time to watch Megan, in her red power suit, walk confidently past the windows. She paused outside the entrance to peruse the chalkboard menu, nodding with appreciation, and then entered the tearoom.

Her smile was strained as Julie greeted her.

"Julie. I couldn't believe it when I heard what you were doing and I just had to check it out. It was certainly a…brave move, opening in such a neighborhood."

Julie's spine stiffened at the affront to her new home turf. Although she'd only lived here a short time, she'd grown to like the neighborhood. There were so many different kinds of people—young, old, black, white, Hispanic, rich, poor, gay, straight. Here, there were people driving cars, riding bicycles and walking.

It was nothing like the Park Cities condo where she'd lived before losing her job, where the homes, the cars and the people had a certain…sameness.

But the last thing she needed to do was get into an argument with a customer. "The neighborhood is on its way up," she said cheerfully as she seated Megan by the window. "I'd recommend the salmon. It's very fresh."

Megan's smile warmed slightly. "Thanks, that sounds terrific. And a glass of Chablis."

Julie placed the order and then noticed something out the window. Several firefighters from across the street were gathering around a grill they'd set up in their driveway, which now had bright flames shooting up into the sky. One of the men carried a huge plate of what looked like ribs. She could only imagine what the air was going to smell like in a few minutes, and it wouldn't put her customers in the mood for salad or quiche.

To top it off, the guys had brought out a boom box, and with the flick of a switch Julie was treated to some particularly bad rap music. It wasn't loud enough to qualify as a nuisance—not that the police would do anything about it if she complained. It was just annoying, something her customers would *never* hear in North Dallas.

She had to do something. She alerted Belinda, asking her to hold down the fort, then left the tearoom and marched across the street. One of the doors to the apparatus room was open, so she entered there rather than ringing the bell at the front door. She found a couple of firefighters carrying a second barbecue grill toward the driveway. One of them was the one who had patched up her hand.

"Carl, right? I need to see your captain, please," she said succinctly. The two men looked at each other.

"He's pretty busy," Carl said uneasily.

"Take me to him now or I'm going higher. I'll go to the chief or the mayor if I have to. This is harassment and it's affecting my livelihood. I'd like to handle this matter quietly." Her threat was implied. If she couldn't resolve this immediately, things would get messy.

Something about her determination killed their cocky grins, and they took her to the captain's office. He was a silver-haired man with a big belly and he seemed to be busy with a great deal of paper on his desk.

"What is it?" he barked. Then he looked up. "Oh, excuse me. Can I help you?"

"You can tell those men out front to please turn down their music and to refrain from blowing their smoke across the street."

"Well, now, I can't order the wind to blow in any particular direction."

"But you can tell the guys to turn down the gangsta rap music."

The captain rolled his eyes. "Dutton," he said to Carl, who was lingering in the doorway to witness the fireworks, "tell whoever's out front to cut it out. Gangsta rap. Jeez."

"Thank you," Julie said, satisfied that at least one problem was solved. She returned to her tearoom, took a deep breath and rejoiced in the fact that at least a few of the tables were occupied.

"What is going on?" Belinda whispered as she passed by carrying a pitcher of raspberry iced tea.

"We're being harassed, that's what. But everything's under control now. Sort of."

Things remained under control for five more

minutes—until two men in overalls and straw hats entered the tearoom, wanting to be seated.

Julie recognized one of the men from the auction. More firefighters. Though their mode of dress was not exactly elegant, she had no choice but to seat the men. She hadn't posted a dress code anywhere, and to turn them away would be inviting a scene.

"Right this way, gentleman," she said with her most gracious smile, thanking her lucky stars that most of the tables in the front section of the restaurant were filled by now. She seated them in the back, where they wouldn't be immediately visible to anyone who was just arriving.

"Oo-ee!" one of them said as he passed by tables of well-heeled diners. "Ain't this sump'n fancy."

"Kinda reminds me of that whorehouse we visited in Nevada," the other one said, earning several outraged stares.

Julie was dying a thousand deaths, but she'd be damned if she'd let them see she was ruffled. She seated them and handed them each a menu. "Can I get your drink orders, gentlemen? How about some peach or raspberry iced tea or perhaps a glass of chardonnay?"

"Got any beer?"

"No, I'm sorry, we don't serve beer."

"Shame. Bring us some Cokes."

"Yes, sir. Your server will be right with you to tell you about today's specials."

For the next few minutes the men talked in loud voices, scratched themselves and belched. But their waitress treated them just like any other customers and they had to order if they wanted to stay. When their food arrived, they got considerably quieter.

"I think they like the food," Belinda observed.

Another battle won.

"Do you know if Mom's coming?" Belinda asked. Julie had made a point of inviting her parents. She knew her father wouldn't want to come. Aside from the fact he would hate this kind of place, he rarely left the house these days. But she'd thought maybe her mother might want to see what she'd done.

"She's not coming," Julie said. "She had to work."

"Oh, you'd think she could have taken time off just this once. How often do her daughters open a tearoom?"

"I don't think she really understands what we're doing here," Julie said, but her mother's lack of interest still stung.

"She doesn't try to understand," Belinda said. "Hey, look who's here."

Tony. For some reason, every bit of self-confidence Julie had been nursing deserted her. She'd invited him, of course, but she hadn't been sure he would come. His fellow firefighters would see it as a betrayal. In fact, they'd given him a real hard time about his friendship—relationship—with her.

And yet here he was. It was heartwarming to see him walk through the door, but scary, too. If her grand opening bombed, she didn't want him, of all people, to witness it.

Priscilla was with him. Julie greeted the two of them with a stiff smile. "Your brethren have been doing their best to spoil my grand opening."

"Oh, yeah. We saw." Tony nodded behind him, indicating the barbecue party across the street. "Just ignore them."

"It's pretty hard. Every time the door opens, I get a whiff of burning pork."

"Well, even if those guys are being jerks," said Priscilla, "we're here to support you."

Julie put a hand to her forehead. "I'm sorry, I shouldn't be so grumpy." She grabbed some menus and led them toward the back so they could see for themselves what she had to contend with.

"Bud." Priscilla greeted one of the men with a nod. "Didn't you tell me you wouldn't set foot in a tearoom? Charlie. Nice outfit."

"Traitors," the one called Bud said under his breath.

Julie seated the newcomers a couple of tables away from the straw-hat duo so they couldn't easily trade barbs.

"I can't believe they're being so mean," Priscilla said. "Those guys are normally pretty nice."

"They're behaving now," Julie said. "Once they got their food and realized it was good." She took drink orders and then said, "Thank you for coming. I know you're risking the wrath of your coworkers."

"We're trying to be good neighbors," Tony said.

"He just wants the free dessert," Priscilla added. "But I'm *dying* to try the food. I heard André Le Croix is working for you."

"He is," Julie confirmed. At an exorbitant salary, too. But if people liked the food as much as she hoped, it would be worth every penny. "Enjoy your meal. And please let me know if there's anything I can do better."

For the next little while she was too busy to think as she paused to chat with customers at each table. She hadn't drawn the crowd she'd hoped for, but it was early days yet.

Eloisa seemed to be doing well. She wasn't taking lunch orders, as she wouldn't be able to understand or answer questions about the food. But she was delivering and clearing plates, refilling water and tea and doing so with grace and poise.

An older matron signaled Julie, who hurried to her table. "Yes, Mrs. Blankenship. What can I do for you?"

"You know me?" she asked, surprised. "I wasn't aware we'd had the pleasure. Although you do look familiar."

"I used to work at Lochinvar's," Julie admitted.

"Oh, of course. Well, I was just a little curious about this place when I got the invitation. I didn't realize it would be such a long drive."

"I appreciate your taking the time to give us a try," Julie said diplomatically. "Are you enjoying the food?"

"I found the chicken a little dry but otherwise very passable."

Julie remembered that Mrs. Blankenship always complained about the food at Lochinvar's. *Passable* was a high compliment.

"I'll pass your comments along to my chef." His reputation as well as hers was riding on the success of Belinda's. Of course, he'd paid more for the raw ingredients than she'd budgeted—more than she'd been accustomed to paying when she'd managed Lochinvar's. But he was a genius. She'd tasted the chicken herself and had found it to be perfection.

A younger woman rushed up to the table. "Mother, you'd better come. The police are towing your car!"

Chapter Eleven

"What?" Julie said at the same time as Mrs. Blankenship.

"They said the meter was expired."

"Oh, for heaven's sake, half those meters on Jefferson don't work and they're *never* enforced."

"Well, the cops are out today in numbers," the young woman said. "A ticket I could understand, but towing?"

Julie stalked outside, and sure enough a tow truck down the block was dragging a gold Cadillac out of its parking space. Farther down, she could see another tow truck. Ah, and the smell of burning pork, stronger than ever.

Julie could throw a fit, but what good would that do? The police had the right to enforce parking laws, though she suspected their sudden attention to the area surrounding Belinda's was not coincidental.

For the rest of the afternoon, Julie waited for another shoe to drop. But she heard nothing more from the firefighters. The men in their straw hats paid for their meals and even left a hefty tip—and they looked a little ashamed as they made their exit. By three o'clock, when the last customer left, the dessert case was nearly cleared out and everyone was exhausted.

But it was over. She'd survived her grand opening.

She'd been wrong about the last customer leaving, though. One remained.

Tony had been lurking in the back, nursing a cup of coffee and lingering over his apple-pecan pie long after Priscilla had left.

Now he approached the cash register, where Julie was closing out the day's receipts. "If you have a couple more desserts, I'll buy them to take home. The pie I had was incredible."

"Thank you. I'm surprised to see you're still here."

"I stuck around in case any more of my coworkers decided to have fun at your expense. Plus, I enjoyed watching everything you've worked so hard for coming together."

"At least your buddies didn't give me any more trouble. But thanks for watching out for me." He looked so handsome in his creased khakis and starched shirt. She couldn't recall ever seeing him quite so dressed up. He'd gotten a haircut, too, just as in her fantasy.

Her heart did its mad flutter as she boxed up a couple of desserts. She added some chocolate cookies for Jasmine.

"Were your parents impressed with what you've done?"

"I invited them, but they couldn't make it."

"They didn't come to the grand opening?" Tony asked, surprised. "I mean, your mother owns the place."

"My mom had to work, and my dad doesn't go anywhere without her. He can't drive himself." Julie tried to filter the hurt out of her voice. Her parents had never understood Julie's ambition or Belinda's aspirations to attend "some hoity-toity school in the east," as they put it.

"I invited my dad to my graduation from the fire academy," Tony said. "But he didn't show."

She squeezed his hand in commiseration. "I guess our parents do the best they can."

A baby's cry coming from the kitchen reminded Julie she had another big problem to contend with.

Eloisa and Josephina.

Tony's head swiveled, his attention drawn by the sound. "Is that a baby?"

"Yes. Tony, you speak Spanish, right?"

"Yeah, sure. Why?"

"That woman who just came out of the kitchen with the baby is Eloisa. Could you explain to her that I'm very happy with her work and I'd like her to continue with me? But she's going to have to fill out papers. And she absolutely must find child care. I don't want to be hard-hearted, but I can't have a crying baby here."

"Sure, I can talk to her."

After Eloisa had finished tending to the baby, he motioned for her to join him at a table. She protested at first—she wanted to keep working. She intended to work until there was no more work left to do and she wasn't too proud to get her hands dirty. Her determination to do her job well made Julie think of herself when she was first out in the working world. She had always worked twice as hard as anyone else, asking questions, finding out what it would take to get a raise or promotion and then following instructions to the letter.

Tony, ever persuasive, took a heavy bus tray from Eloisa and set it down. The two settled at a table and carried on a conversation in rapid-fire Spanish, of which Julie could not understand a word.

She wished she'd paid better attention in her high school Spanish classes. She would dearly love to know what they were saying to each other.

Julie continued to count receipts, watching the two from the corner of her eye. Every so often Eloisa would point to Julie. And then she started crying, and Tony patted her on the shoulder.

Julie couldn't help feeling a twinge of jealousy. Eloisa was very pretty. And Tony, being a firefighter, had that rescue gene in him. Would he take her home and feed her?

After a few minutes more, Eloisa came over to Julie and hugged her. "Thank you, Miss Julie. I be here tomorrow early for papers." She looked uncertainly at Tony.

"She needs bus fare to get home," Tony said. "I can cover it…"

"No, no, her share of the tips is more than enough

to get her home." Julie pulled some ones from the petty-cash box and handed them to Eloisa, making a quick note for bookkeeping purposes.

Finally she managed to get Eloisa out the door. There was only a little bit of work left.

"You did really well today," Tony said. "Grace under pressure. And I liked the food. I actually ate quiche. It's not much different than pot pie."

"It's a miracle."

He laughed. But then he sobered. "What you did for Eloisa was generous."

"She's a good worker and a fast learner. I'd be stupid to turn her away."

"She doesn't have any references—her previous employer skipped town. She doesn't even have a permanent address and she speaks very little English."

"I was desperate for another waitress. I'm not a saint."

"Not every woman would be so open-minded. She's in a very bad place. Her husband left her, disappeared, took all their money. And then she lost her job when Dollar Olé closed."

Steam nearly came out of Julie's ears. She was tired of hearing about men who didn't take responsibility for their children. "All the more reason for me to help her out."

It amazed her how little she'd even thought of Trey the past few weeks. His betrayal, which only two months ago had devastated her and caused her to cry for days, hardly gave her a twinge now. "I have a good feeling about Eloisa. She just needs a leg up."

She started for the kitchen, but Tony caught her arm and pulled her against him. She resisted at first, but then she yielded, letting him kiss her.

"We should go out and celebrate," he said.

"Oh, Tony, I can't. I have so much… Ah, I wish you wouldn't do that."

He kissed her under her ear. "I've been really good, not bugging you."

"I know. But I've got work to do. It went well today, all things considered, but there are adjustments to make. André is a talented chef, but he's a bear to work for. Marc, his assistant, walked out in a huff a few minutes ago." She forced a smile. "But everything's okay."

"I guess it was a good thing you weren't too busy in the dining room."

"That's one way to look at it." After that flurry of early activity, customers had only trickled in.

"Are you worried?"

"A little. But it's just my first day. I have some ads running next week. And they're doing an article about me on the Oak Cliff Web site. I just have to survive until word of mouth starts to spread."

"It will. The food is really good here. Although I still say you need hamburgers and beer…."

She pulled away, thinking. Had she been too inflexible about her vision for Belinda's? "You know, maybe you're right. How hard would it be to add a hamburger to the menu? And maybe a few microbrewery designer beers."

Tony couldn't believe she would even entertain

the idea. She'd been dead set against it a few weeks earlier. Maybe things were going worse than he thought. "You know, if you need a loan or something, just to tide you over until…"

"Oh, no, no, no. I think that's a very bad way to start off a relationship."

"Why? I trust you. You're good for it."

"Unless the restaurant goes south. No, I already owe a lot of other people money. I don't want to add you to the list." She waved away his concern. "It's okay. Business will pick up next week, and I'll find someone to replace Marc."

"Still, the offer stands. I don't have a boatload of cash, but I have some."

"Thank you, Tony. But no." She looked at her watch. "Isn't Jasmine due home from school right about now?"

"Yeah, I guess I better go. Natalie told me Jasmine's been wearing makeup at school and washing it off before she comes home. We have to have a little chat."

Julie laughed. "Oh, man. Isn't she young for that? I didn't want to wear makeup until I was at least twelve."

"She is so advanced for her age I honestly don't know what to do."

"Man. I don't envy you when she reaches her teens."

It was on the tip of Tony's tongue to mention that, if he had his way, Julie would be Jasmine's stepmom by the time she became a teenager. But he stifled the comment. Priscilla was still coaching him, every chance she got, that he had to give the relationship time and let it grow at its own pace. He always wanted to rush things.

Priscilla still insisted he couldn't be in love with Julie, that it was too soon. Tony wasn't so sure. That ache in his chest every time he saw her and the fact that he shared her doubts and anxiety about the success of the tearoom—what was that if not love?

"Jasmine will be a handful. She just bought her first bra. I can't believe it."

"Wow. Does she really need it?"

"Her mother says she does."

"Do you get along well with your ex?" Julie asked casually.

"Oh, sure. Natalie's great." He toyed with the idea of confessing that Natalie wasn't really his "ex," at least not in the way Julie meant. But he decided now was the wrong time. Maybe tonight.

Julie sent Tony on his way with a smile and a promise, but when she turned back toward her tiny office, her heart was heavy. She'd put on a brave face, but she was worried. Certainly her opening hadn't produced the crowd she'd been hoping for.

She sat down at her desk and started totaling receipts, but her mind was so clouded with doubt she had a hard time making the appropriate entries in her bookkeeping program. She was exhausted. Happy that she'd survived her first day but daunted by the thought that she would have to get up and do it all again tomorrow.

What if she was wrong? What if this neighborhood simply wasn't ready for an upscale tearoom? She'd seen a few of the locals stop, look at the chalkboard with interest, then shake their heads and walk on. Had the prices scared them away? They were a little lower than what Lochinvar's charged for similar fare. But this wasn't Park Cities.

What did she know about running a business, anyway? A year at a tearoom with an established clientele and employees who'd been in the kitchen forever hadn't prepared her for the headaches she was facing at this moment.

She'd known from the beginning that failure was a possibility. But she'd brushed that reality under the rug as much as she could, confident that she could *will* Belinda's into being a success. Having Marc walk out because of André's temperamental outbursts had thrown her for a loop.

By the time she'd finished adding up the receipts, she was more depressed than ever. If she made this amount every day, she might be able to make her first payroll. But there wouldn't be much left for overhead. Worse, she had a balloon payment coming up. She'd been counting on sufficient cash flow to persuade a bank to let her roll it over into a longer-term loan. Now she put her head down on her desk and wept from exhaustion.

Two days later Tony was on duty, digging in to a dinner of grilled sausage, au gratin potatoes, coleslaw and pound cake. "A little heartier than what your girlfriend serves at lunch, I'll bet," said Bing Tate, who could be really annoying when he wanted to be.

Tony refused to be drawn into an argument. "It's good," Tony said. And it was. It was easy to see how some firefighters gained weight. Maybe Priscilla and Julie were on to something with their insistence on eating healthier fare.

The shift was dull. At close to midnight, Tony knew he should try to get some sleep. But he found himself in the fitness area, lifting weights and watching out the window. The last light had gone off in Julie's apartment an hour ago, after he'd spoken to her briefly on the phone to wish her good-night.

Otis joined him, hopping on the treadmill. Oh, joy.

"Got to run off some of those potatoes," he said. "You ever notice how we don't eat anything green around here?"

"You're starting to sound like Priscilla."

"Well, she's right about some things. Ruby says I ought to lose some weight. She doesn't think I'm sexy enough."

Tony didn't care to think about Otis and *sexy* in the same sentence.

"She dragged me to Belinda's yesterday."

"Really?" That was a shock.

"It wasn't half-bad. I could have eaten twice as much food as they put on the plate, but it tasted good."

"The portions are ladylike. On purpose," Tony said.

"Your girlfriend doesn't want men eating there?"

"Not so much. She likes to keep the atmosphere girlie. But a few well-behaved men, that's okay."

Otis laughed. "How's she gonna make any money alienating half the population?"

Tony shook his head. "Good question."

"I noticed she didn't have many customers."

"No."

"You think she'll stay open?"

"I don't know," Tony said. The thought of Julie having to close Belinda's...well, it made his chest ache to imagine her failing. But maybe the new ads and word of mouth would bring in more customers.

"I hope she makes it," Otis said, surprising Tony. "I still miss Brady's. But it's pretty amazing what your Julie's done with the place. I guess she's entitled to have her tearoom."

"I thought you guys wanted to buy her out?"

"We talked to some of the lien holders, but no one can agree on terms, so we're pretty well dead in the water."

There was one avenue the partnership hadn't considered. They could contact Julie's mother. She was the actual owner of the building and the business, after all. As little as the woman seemed to care about Julie's business, she might just accept a wad of cash. But apparently the Brady's Consortium hadn't realized that, and Tony wasn't going to tell them.

Tony's attention was drawn back to the window. A light downstairs. Was Julie up and prowling? He knew she had trouble sleeping sometimes. If she was awake, he would call her again. He liked hearing her voice.

But now he wasn't sure whether he'd seen a light at all. Maybe it was just a reflection from a passing motorist's headlights.

The treadmill wound to a halt, and Otis joined Tony at the window. "What are you starin' at?"

"I thought I saw a light. Shouldn't be any lights on downstairs this time of night. There. I did see something…."

"That's no light," Otis said. "That's a fire!"

Chapter Twelve

Tony had no memory of how he got downstairs, how he got into his turnout gear. Next thing he knew, he was facing Captain Campeon. "Julie's in there. She lives in the apartment above the restaurant. I'm going over on foot." He didn't wait for Campeon's okay. He took off at a dead run, dodging a car that ignored his signal to stop, speed-dialing Julie's number on his cell as he ran.

Her answering machine had picked up by the time he reached the parking lot in back. Maybe she wasn't home. But where would she be?

He banged on the separate door that led to her apartment. "Julie, pick up the phone!" he yelled into his cell. Then he shouted, "Julie, answer the door!" He got no response to either demand.

What if she had already been overcome by smoke? He had no way of knowing how advanced the fire was, but if they could see flames through the window, it might have been burning for hours.

Both doors in back were steel. No hope of getting

through them without serious tools. Every window was barred—the place was like Fort Knox. She had no fire escape, though Tony had at least bought her a rope ladder. But a ladder would do her no good if she was unconscious.

He'd made a stupid mistake arriving without any tools. Fueled by anger and frustration with himself, he ran back to the front of the building. The engine had pulled across the street, its red-and-white lights flashing eerily in the darkness. Ethan and McCrae were busy cutting through the front door with a K-12 rotary saw.

Tony peered through the windows. He couldn't see flames, but that might be because the tearoom was full of smoke.

He again reported to Campeon, who was now the official Incident Commander. "I can't raise her. Request permission to take a ladder to an upstairs window."

"Affirmative," Campeon said with his usual military precision. "Take Granger."

Tony snagged Otis and filled him in on their assignment as he pulled a wall ladder off Engine 59. He heard the door give way. Glass shattered. Smoke poured out. They got the ladder in place in record time. With his breathing apparatus on, his ax ready, Tony climbed faster than he'd climbed any ladder in his life. Otis trailed behind, his breathing labored. "Wait for me, eager beaver. Man, I got to get in better shape."

Wait, hell. With one sharp crack with his ax Tony

tore through the window screen and glass. In moments, he was through. "Julie!"

He was relieved to see the smoke was only a thin haze on the second floor. The bedroom was empty except for a chest of drawers. Still no bed. He opened the door into the living room, where the smoke was a bit thicker—and thicker still toward the door leading downstairs.

God, what if she'd been downstairs, tending to some detail? Maybe she hadn't been able to sleep and she'd gone downstairs to check on something?

Then he saw her. She was lying on the couch, fully clothed. "Julie!" he bellowed and he reached her in two strides.

She jolted awake. "Huh?"

Tony's knees nearly buckled with relief. "There's a fire downstairs. You have to get out."

She whipped her head around, still a bit disoriented. "A fire? In the *tearoom?*" She was vertical in a flash and heading toward the door. He tried to snag her arm as she passed, but his gloves made him clumsy and he missed her.

"Not that way!" he yelled. "The window."

But it was too late. She opened the door, and hot smoke billowed in from downstairs.

He yanked her away from the opening, which would help ventilate downstairs but wasn't too healthy for them up here. "The window!"

She looked at him as if he were crazy. "My tearoom is on fire. I'm not going to jump out the window like a scared rabbit."

"It's being taken care of."

"But how…?" She paused to cough.

"Are you coming or do I have to drag you?" Tony heard Otis reporting their situation to IC. She made a move toward the door again, but Tony held fast to her arm.

"My tearoom," she tried again.

So did Tony. He didn't want to have to drag her out the window, but he would if he had to. "Your safety is more important than a tearoom."

Her direct look challenged him, and then she slumped in defeat. Thank God.

"There's no one else here, is there?"

"No, of course not." Coughing now, she allowed herself to be led to the bedroom window, casting only a glazed glance at the broken glass on the floor.

Tony went out first, then helped Julie. "Careful, there's some sharp glass."

She made no response, but she was agile enough on the ladder to climb down on her own. Tony was there to prevent her from falling, but she didn't need his help. Otis followed.

Tony led Julie along the sidewalk, well out of danger. He pulled off his breathing gear. "Stay here. Don't move. And stay out of the way until we're sure this thing's out."

She peered through the darkness toward her building. "I don't even see any smoke down here. Tony, what happened?"

"We'll know more in a bit." He left her alone— he had no choice. He had a job to do, and his job wasn't to comfort her. But Peterson and Kevin Sinclair, on paramedic duty, were heading for her, so she wouldn't be alone for long.

When he reported back to Captain Campeon, he was relieved to learn the fire was under control. The flames had been limited to the storage room and office area. But the firefighters' work wasn't done. They had to continue spraying down hot spots and tearing into walls and ceilings to make sure every single cinder was cold and dead.

Civilians always complained about the damage firefighters did, even during a small fire—the water, ashy footprints everywhere and especially the holes—whether they were made for ventilation or to check for fire inside walls and ceilings, where it usually traveled. Tony could only imagine what Julie would have to say. But better some superficial damage than to walk away too soon, before the fire was truly out.

The captain had no further tasks for him other than to direct traffic and keep people away, which normally wasn't a problem for a small fire at this time of night. Still, there were always a few "blue lighters" who monitored the fire department's radio and came to watch.

After directing a car to maneuver around the engine, he glanced back to where he'd left Julie. She was gone.

"Damn. Otis, I'll be back in a second."

Otis gave him a knowing nod. "Okay. But if you're looking for your girl, she's over there."

"What?" He looked where Otis pointed. And there was Julie, practically spitting nails in the captain's face.

Not good. He knew people got emotional when they saw their homes or their businesses in flames. They said and did things they didn't mean. But it wasn't safe to lose your cool in front of Campeon. The guy had the compassion of a block of ice.

Tony knew Julie wasn't thinking straight. Damn, he should have made sure she was safely with the paramedics before leaving her.

He approached Julie and the captain cautiously, just as Julie was yelling, "I demand that you get those men out of my restaurant immediately. Just *look* what they're doing! Who's going to pay for this mess? The fire is out, why are they still stomping around in there, breaking things?"

"Ma'am," the captain said, "until that fire is out, you don't own that restaurant—I do."

Tony touched her shoulder. "Julie…"

She whirled around, not appearing happy to see him in the least. "What?"

Campeon grimaced. "Veracruz, control your girlfriend."

Tony tried to take her arm, intending to nudge her back to a safer vantage point. Though it looked as if the fire was out, it was wise not to draw premature conclusions.

Julie shook him off. "Control me? Look, just because you're sleeping with me doesn't mean you can *control* me."

Tony wasn't sure whether Campeon was about to explode or burst out laughing.

Bing Tate overheard the exchange and paused in his task of putting the saw back on the engine. He flashed an evil grin.

"I thought all along we sent in the wrong man," he said to Tony but loud enough that anyone on the whole block could hear. "If you'd given the job to me, this place'd still be Brady's."

Tony had never wanted to sock a man in the nose as bad as he did at that moment. Tate, not one of his favorite people to begin with, had timed his barb to inflict the maximum damage—when Julie was already in an emotional state, watching her tearoom turned into a shambles.

Julie narrowed her gaze. "What are you talking about? Tony, what's he talking about?"

"Hey," Campeon barked. "This isn't *The Young and the Restless*. You," he said to Julie, "get away from my fire and let me do my job. I want you across the street. I'll tell you when it's safe for you to reenter the building and I better not see you again until then or I'll have you arrested. And *you*—" he turned on Tony "—get back to your job!"

"Yes, sir."

Something in Campeon's voice made Julie back down. She shuffled away, but she couldn't resist one final barb. "Guess you guys got what you wanted after all. Congratulations."

Oh, man, did he have some explaining to do.

As he returned to his job of directing traffic, Tony

saw more bad news. Roark Epperson's car had pulled up behind the engine. It was standard procedure to call in an investigator on any fire that involved property damage. But the fact they'd called in Epperson—the big gun—meant someone really did suspect arson.

At least Tony knew the investigator would be thorough.

First making sure the captain was busy with other things, Tony met Epperson as he exited his SUV. They shook hands.

"What's going on here?" Epperson asked casually, still shaking off residual drowsiness. He'd probably been warm in his bed less than an hour ago.

"I can't tell you much. What I heard is that the fire was confined to two small rooms in the back of the restaurant. I was never inside, except on the second floor to get the owner out of the building."

"That woman who destroyed Brady's?" Epperson asked, cocking one eyebrow. "She was upstairs?"

Tony knew resentment still ran high among some firefighters. He also knew this wasn't the time or place to try to defend Julie. "That's the one. She's over there if you want to talk to her." Tony nodded across the street, where Julie had finally succumbed and allowed the paramedics to give her a chair and some oxygen. "But trust me, she doesn't know anything. I had to break a window to get to her." He nodded toward where Otis was taking down the ladder. "She was in a dead sleep and had no idea what was going on."

Epperson seemed a bit more alert as he pulled a notebook out of his back pocket and started taking notes. "You let her get dressed?"

"What? Oh, no, she was like that."

"Shoes, too?"

"She must have fallen asleep watching TV or something."

"Is her business doing well?" Epperson asked, again too casually.

Tony pinched the bridge of his nose. "She just opened a couple of days ago. So if you're thinking insurance fraud or something, you're barking up the wrong tree. Julie had nothing to do with setting the fire."

The investigator studied Tony. "Oh, wait a minute. You're the one who tried to get her to change her mind about Brady's by…"

"Damn! The department grapevine is about to strangle me."

Epperson grinned. "If you're sleeping with her, I can't believe a word you say, even if you are a brother." And he sauntered toward the soggy tearoom, leaving Tony cursing silently and wondering if he'd just gotten Julie in a whole lot of trouble.

Julie did need money. He knew she had a loan payment coming due before long. Still, it was utterly ridiculous to think she would destroy something she loved so much. But Epperson didn't know Julie. And the property owner was often the first suspect in an arson case.

Damn.

NOW THAT THE SHOCK had worn off, Julie felt sick to her stomach. Her beloved tearoom, up in flames. They wouldn't even let her see the damage. Although the building was intact and there was no more smoke or fire, she could only imagine the damage inside. They wouldn't let her near the place. It was *her* tearoom, her building, but the firefighters were treating her like some pesky mosquito.

She could only watch from across the street while two paramedics hovered over her. They seemed sincere in wanting to comfort her, but at this pointshe didn't trust anyone's motives. They were probably suppressing the urge to dance a jig because Belinda's was burning. They probably thought it was what she deserved for destroying their precious bar.

Then there was Tony. The more she tried not to think about what that other fireman had said, the more it plagued her.

We sent in the wrong man.... If you'd given the job to me, this place'd still be Brady's.

What exactly had he meant by that? If she struggled, she could probably come up with an innocent explanation. But the play of emotions across Tony's face had said it all. First he'd looked stricken and then undeniably guilty.

So Tony had been "sent" to deal with her somehow. To reason with her? To intimidate her? He'd definitely tried the first, not the second. But somehow she suspected there was a lot more to it than that.

The determined approach of a strange man in

civilian clothes ended her speculations for the moment. She'd spotted his arrival a few minutes earlier. Though he hadn't been wearing any protective gear, he'd been allowed to roam freely and talk to anyone. Now, apparently, he'd decided to talk to her.

She didn't feel good about this.

She stood up as he drew closer, so he wouldn't tower over her. He still topped her by half a head. And talk about intimidation! Though he wasn't half-bad looking, the steely look in his eyes scared the hell out of her.

"Roark Epperson," he said, extending his hand. "I'm an arson investigator." The way he said it, it sounded like *ahs-sun investigatah*. Definitely not from around here.

She shook his hand distractedly, riveted by a sudden realization. "You think my fire was caused by arson?" The thought hadn't even occurred to her. Though she had no idea what had caused the fire, she'd assumed it was something like faulty wiring or a short—even spontaneous combustion, what with all the cooking oils and paper towels. Arson had never entered her mind.

"I won't know until I take a closer look. But don't worry, it's standard procedure to call in an arson investigator when the cause of a fire can't be easily determined. Many turn out to be accidental."

"But not all."

"That's what keeps me employed. Let's go inside the station, where I can get a cup of coffee and we can sit down." It wasn't an invitation, it was an order.

And though only a few minutes ago Julie had been feeling feisty and argumentative, all the starch had gone out of her now.

Arson. Who would hate her enough to want to burn down her restaurant? She wasn't winning a popularity contest with any number of people at the moment. But she couldn't imagine any of them taking their anger so far. A little graffiti was one thing. Burning down a building was something else entirely. Besides, who would have had access?

Roark Epperson brought her a cup of coffee in a chipped mug. "I added some milk. Hope you don't mind."

"That's fine." She took a sip. But when it landed in her stomach, it immediately started to burn, so she set the mug aside. "You didn't grow up in Texas," she said.

He smiled. "No. Boston."

"Ah, that's why you sound like a long-lost Kennedy."

He shrugged boyishly. But then he was all business. He asked her a few preliminary questions, establishing her identity and her status as the daughter of the building's owner, plus the fact she operated a business downstairs and lived above it. He asked who had locked up the restaurant, who'd been the last to leave. The answer to both questions was Julie herself.

"Belinda's has only been open…how long?"

She sighed. "Three days." Not even long enough for her to find out if she was any good as a restaurateur. "Oh, God, my employees. My sister! She quit a really good job at a steak house to wait tables at Belinda's. And poor Eloisa."

Epperson ignored her outburst. "When officers Veracruz and Granger entered your apartment to alert you, you were asleep—is that right?"

"Yes."

"On the sofa?"

"Yes. I don't actually have a real bed."

"So you went to sleep fully clothed?"

She looked down at herself. "I guess so. I honestly don't remember. But I've been working some ridiculous hours." She'd pretty well fallen asleep standing up in the shower the day before. Only the blast of cold when the hot water ran out had revived her.

"And last night, when did you fall asleep?"

"It would have been this morning. I know I was up past midnight. But the exact time…I just don't know."

"Were you with anyone last night?"

"No. I was alone."

He made a note, and she wondered why he cared about her clothes or her personal habits.

"Do you have any enemies, Ms. Polk?" he asked. The tone of his question was alarming.

"*Enemies* is a strong word. There are a few people who aren't happy with me right now, starting with all the Oak Cliff firefighters and cops who used to frequent Brady's. But despite the…animosity, I'd hardly consider any of them suspects. Besides, no one broke in. Did they?"

"How would you know? You didn't go out by the back door."

"I have an alarm. I'd have known if anyone broke through a door or window."

"You have a fire alarm, too, right?"

"Yes. And sprinklers." She felt sick at the thought of all those sprinklers soaking her beautiful tearoom.

"But you didn't hear the fire alarm."

She thought back to when Tony had awakened her. Was the alarm going off? Not the smoke alarm in her apartment. That thing was loud enough to wake the dead. But the one in the tearoom? Surely she would have heard that after she woke up. "I don't remember hearing anything. But I sleep hard and I was disoriented to wake up to the smoke—and two men dressed like aliens telling me to get up and jump out the window."

More notes. Epperson's face gave away nothing.

"Any disgruntled employees?"

"No one has worked long enough for me, to become disgruntled. Oh, well, I take that back. One of the kitchen staff quit the first day. But he was mad at my head chef, not me." Still, she provided Marc's name. Belinda would not be pleased.

"Anyone who applied for a job that you *didn't* hire?"

"Sure, there were lots of applicants. But no one stands out as a likely person to bear a grudge."

"What about ex-husbands, ex-boyfriends?"

"No ex-husbands…" She hesitated. Not in a million years could she imagine Trey or any of his friends or family stooping to something as sordid as arson. But Trey had been angry with her when she'd called off the wedding. Unreasonably angry.

"There is a boyfriend, I take it."

She told Epperson, as briefly as possible, of her broken engagement, and when he pressed her, she gave him Trey's name. "But there's no way. I mean, really. I haven't heard even a peep out of him or anyone connected to him since I moved out of the town house I was renting from his parents."

More scribbles in the notebook.

"You aren't going to talk to him, are you?" She couldn't bear the thought of them gloating over her failure. She didn't think they would deliberately harm her, but they weren't above reveling in her misfortune.

"If it's arson, I'll be talking with everyone until I find who did it. And that's a promise."

Julie thought it sounded more like a threat.

Chapter Thirteen

The sky was starting to lighten when Julie exited the fire station. Across the street, the firefighters were folding their hoses and preparing to retreat. Finally she could get in and see the damage.

But the odious Captain Campeon soon disabused her of that notion. "For now, we're treating this building as if it were a crime scene."

"The whole building? My apartment, too?"

"I'm afraid so. Someone can escort you upstairs to collect a few personal belongings if you'd like."

"Yes, I'd like."

A FIREFIGHTER WHOSE name tag identified him as K. Sinclair escorted her inside. Epperson grumbled about letting more people tromp through the scene of the fire, but in the end he let Julie pass. He warned her not to touch anything.

Julie took one step inside, skidded to a halt and tried not to faint. "Oh, my God!" It looked as though a herd of dirty, wet buffalo had stampeded through.

Tables and chairs were overturned, fine table linens trampled and everything was soaking wet. Yet she could see no evidence of anything burned except toward the very back, near the door that led to her office and the storeroom, where one wall and the ceiling bore ugly black scorch marks. "Oh. My. God."

"It's not as bad as it could be," Sinclair said. "We managed to keep the fire confined to the store—"

"Not as bad? The only way it could be worse would be if the building had actually burned to the ground. Everything is ruined." She looked around again, noting the sodden curtains and the smoke-stained upholstery on her chairs.

There was no point in arguing with anyone about this. The only person who would really get it was her insurance adjuster. Thank God she hadn't cut corners where that was concerned. Given the fact her building was a historic landmark, she'd had to pay higher rates. But her policy allowed for full replacement value of everything, including contents.

Upstairs in her apartment, there didn't appear to be any damage. But everything smelled like smoke, including the clothing she quickly packed up to take—who knew where? She'd have to return to her parents' house. They wouldn't be too thrilled. In fact, she had a pretty good idea what they'd say when they learned of the fire. They'd advise her to collect on the insurance and put the building up for sale. Given that her mother was the actual owner of the building, Julie realized she might be forced to do just that.

The firefighters would win.

She collected a few toiletries, her purse, cell phone and car keys. Unfortunately Roark Epperson was waiting for her downstairs, his hand outstretched. "Your car is part of the investigation just now, so I'll need your keys. I also need a phone number where you can be reached."

It just got worse and worse, but Julie gave him her cell number and handed over her keys. "How am I supposed to get home without a car?"

Tony, lurking nearby, stepped forward. "I thought you'd come stay with me. I'll be off duty in a few minutes."

She wasn't ready to face Tony. She was emotional, exhausted and she knew he'd been dishonest with her. She wasn't prepared to deal with that reality just now. Not until she found out exactly what that Tate guy had meant by "We sent in the wrong man."

She curbed her urge to fly off the handle. Getting emotional wouldn't help matters. "I don't think that's a good idea."

He led her outside, where they could talk privately. "No obligation, okay? You don't even have to talk to me if you don't want to."

"Look, Tony, I'm too tired and too upset to think rationally. I need to call my employees and let them know what's happened. Then I need to sleep."

"If this is about what Bing Tate said…"

"It is."

"I can explain. It's not what it looks like."

"Tell me, Tony, what does it look like?"

"If you'll let me explain—"

"Stop. Just stop. I can't take any more in right now. I mean, arson. Who could hate me that much?"

"Epperson's a good investigator. He'll figure out what caused the fire and who did it, if it's arson."

She squeezed her eyes shut, willing herself not to cry. She didn't have the luxury of falling apart now.

Tony put an arm around her. "Don't cry, babe. I know how much you loved Belinda's, but—"

"Don't put it in the past tense," she interrupted, pulling herself together. "I still love Belinda's and I'm reopening as soon as humanly possible. And if someone deliberately torched my building, I'll see him in jail."

In front of Belinda's, a pickup truck with a camper top had pulled up to the curb that the fire engine had just vacated. A woman in dark pants and a Dallas Fire Rescue golf shirt hopped out, greeting several of the men milling around with a lazy wave.

"Who's that?" Julie asked Tony.

"Captain Betsy Wingate. Dog handler."

"Dog handler?"

The woman opened the back of her truck, and a gorgeous black Labrador retriever bounded out, eager to play.

"Accelerant-sniffing dog. Come on, we need to clear the area. You can come over to the fire station and call someone to pick you up, if you absolutely refuse to come home with me. Or if you can wait a few minutes till I get off, I'll take you to your parents' house."

She didn't want Tony to see the run-down neighborhood where she'd grown up or the tiny place her parents and Belinda called home. She knew she shouldn't be embarrassed by her humble beginnings, but she was.

"Can I sleep on your couch?" she asked in a small voice, conceding defeat. She was just too wiped out to figure her way out of anything.

"If that's what you want, sure." Back at the station, he found his keys and handed them to her. "Sleep wherever you feel most comfortable. I'll try not to wake you when I get home."

Tony had hoped Julie would relent and sleep in his bed. But when he arrived at his house a few minutes later, he found her on the living room sofa wearing a polka-dot tank top and matching boxer shorts. Her hair was wet and tangled from a recent shower. It looked as if she hadn't even combed it. And she was already in a deep sleep.

His chest ached just looking at her. She seemed so peaceful. If there was any way he could have spared her from the pain tonight had brought... But, no, he was partly to blame. He should have been honest with her from the beginning.

If only that idiot Tate hadn't gone and blabbed. He hadn't gone into details, but obviously he'd said enough that Julie could fit together the missing pieces. Tony should have listened to Priscilla and told Julie the truth. Come to think of it, he never should have agreed in the first place to any half-baked scheme to derail the tearoom plans.

Tony had showered at the station, so he shed his clothes and climbed directly into bed. But he couldn't sleep. Though Julie had shared this bed only a couple of times, it felt empty when he knew she was right in the next room. After thirty frustrating minutes of tossing and turning, he got up, dressed and went to the kitchen to find something to eat. Julie was still sound asleep.

He called down to the station and asked if anyone knew anything more about the cause of the fire. The A shift was probably keeping an eye on things. But all anyone would tell him was that the accelerant-sniffing dog had gone home and Epperson was still on the scene collecting samples and taking pictures.

Figured. Roark Epperson never did anything halfway.

Tony knew it looked suspicious finding Julie fully clothed, her shoes already on, conveniently asleep on the sofa—ready to make a run for it if the fire got too close before she was "rescued." But what possible motive would she have? That tearoom was her dream. She had put everything into it. Every penny she had, every ounce of energy and imagination. She wouldn't let a slow start discourage her for long.

A throat clearing alerted Tony to the fact that he was no longer alone. Julie stood in the kitchen doorway, looking deliciously rumpled, those polka-dot boxers showing miles of slender leg.

He recovered enough from the sensual jolt to speak actual words. "Hey, you're awake." Brilliant observation.

"Can I have some of that coffee?"

"I'll get it for you," Tony said. "Sit down. Want some breakfast?"

"I don't think I can eat."

He poured her a cup and gave it to her black, the way he knew she liked it. He loved knowing little things about her—what toppings she ordered on her pizza, the kind of movies she liked to see, her favorite color. He'd always wanted to have a girlfriend to share private jokes with. And memories.

They'd only recently started to feel comfortable around each other, and he'd been looking forward to new discoveries, sharing new experiences, building those memories. But the whole thing would end prematurely if he couldn't convince Julie that his attempts to get to know her, to flirt with her, to seduce her, had been one hundred percent sincere—even if he'd had an ulterior motive.

Julie took an appreciative sip of her coffee, but it didn't help. She had never felt so wretched. Her entire life was falling apart, and how fair was that when it had already fallen apart once this year? Her restaurant was a shambles. Her boyfriend had lied to her. And to top if off, she was suspected of being an arsonist.

"Is there anything I can do to help?" Tony asked.

"Shoot me. Put me out of my misery."

"Now don't talk like that. You've faced some tough challenges before and you're not a quitter. You'll rebuild and you'll make Belinda's even better than before."

She sighed. Last night she'd been mad and spoken some brave words, but this morning it was hard to even think about rebuilding. "I wish I could believe that. André quit when I called him. He said he had another offer and he was taking it."

"So you'll hire another chef."

"When I think about how hard it was the first time…"

"You'll have more help this time. You don't have to do everything by yourself, you know." He watched her intently. "You sure you don't want something to eat?"

Maybe she needed something in her stomach after all. "Could I have some toast?"

"I can do that." He jumped to his feet and got busy.

She looked at her watch. "I better get dressed. Belinda's picking me up any minute." She turned, but Tony caught her hand and stopped her.

"Julie, don't leave. Stay here. Let me take care of you. Let me help you. I know you're having some doubts about me, but we can work them out."

"I don't know, Tony…."

"I'll tell you the whole story. But it's not what Tate made it sound like."

"So you weren't sent on a mission to seduce me and then convince me to reopen Brady's?"

Long pause as he put some white bread in the toaster. "Well, yeah, I was."

Her heart plummeted. If that was the case, it was every bit as bad as she feared. "Then there's nothing else to say."

The doorbell rang, and Julie jumped up to answer it, thinking it was Belinda. But when she opened the door, she found Jasmine instead.

The little girl smiled broadly. "Oh, hi, Julie." And she breezed in, a stuffed backpack slung over one shoulder. Apparently finding a woman in pajamas at her father's house wasn't an unusual circumstance. Something to consider.

"Jas, what are you doing here?" asked Tony, coming out of the kitchen.

"You said if I came over early today, you'd take me and Samantha to Six Flags."

"I didn't mean at the crack of dawn."

"Mom wanted to drop me off on her way to work. Hey, Julie, will you come to my room? I want to show you something."

"Jas," Tony said, "this isn't a good time to bug Julie. She had a fire last night."

Jasmine gasped. "That's horrible. The tearoom?"

"Yeah," Julie said.

"Was it bad? I didn't even get to eat there yet."

"She's gonna reopen. Don't worry," Tony said, sounding a lot more optimistic than Julie felt.

"Please, just come to my room for a minute." Jasmine took Julie's hand and dragged her, but she didn't really mind. Jasmine was so sweet; such an odd mixture, a little kid who desperately wanted to be older.

Tony shrugged helplessly as if to say he was no match for a female, even a pint-size one.

"What are you going to show me?" Julie asked as the little girl tugged her down the hall toward her room.

"Shh," Jasmine said. "It's a secret." She led Julie into her room and closed the door. The room was a pink-and-purple haven for a little girl, with stuffed animals and dolls peeking from every corner—as well as a poster of the latest teenaged heartthrob.

Jasmine opened the drawer to her bedside table and pulled out a red velvet pouch, which she opened reverently. She extracted a heart, about an inch wide, made of intricately worked Mexican silver. She looked at it for a moment, as if composing her thoughts, then handed it to Julie.

"It's an antique. My great-grandma brought it from Mexico."

Even Julie, who knew little about Mexican silver, could tell the piece was an example of exquisite craftsmanship. "It's lovely."

"My grandma, Helena, gave it to me before she died, for safekeeping."

"Your father's mother?"

Jasmine nodded, and Julie was surprised. She hadn't realized Tony's mother was deceased. Tony didn't talk much about his parents. Julie had gleaned enough information to know his home situation had been less than ideal and sometimes painful, so she hadn't pressed him for details.

"She died last year," Jasmine offered. "She had a bad liver."

"She must have loved and trusted you a lot to give you such a beautiful thing," Julie said, still studying the heart.

"But it's not mine to keep. It's supposed to get passed down to the wife of the oldest son in each family. Nana Helena told me to give it to whoever my dad gets married to."

"That's a lovely tradition," Julie said, wondering where all this was going and afraid to speculate.

"I want to give it to you."

Julie looked up, startled, to see Jasmine staring at her with unabashed adoration.

"My dad's had a lot of girlfriends," she said bluntly. "And every time I meet a new one, the first thing I think is, 'Could I give her Nana's heart?' And I always said, 'No way.' Until you. I think you're the one who's meant to have it."

Julie was so touched her eyes filled with tears. She and Jasmine hadn't spent much time together yet, and Julie felt unworthy of the child's affection and faith. She opened her arms, and Jasmine came in for a killer hug, the kind you remember always.

"I'm so honored," Julie said, meaning it. "But I think this is a little premature. We don't know what the future will bring." Boy, was that an understatement.

Jasmine pulled away so she could look at Julie

with her big, earnest brown eyes, so much like her father's. "There will be a wedding," she said with unwavering certainty. "But I want you to take the heart now."

Julie knew it wasn't right to take the heirloom when her future with Tony was in limbo. Still, she sensed Jasmine's determination. "I'll take it for now," she said. "But only for safekeeping and with the understanding that I might have to give it back."

Jasmine smiled. "You won't."

"Jazzy!" Tony called down the hall. "Let Julie go. Her sister is here to pick her up."

And here Julie was, still in her pajamas.

"Don't show it to my dad, whatever you do," Jasmine said. "It's a secret—only the ladies in the family know about it. Okay?"

"Sure, okay." Who was she to mess with a family tradition so complex? "But I was wondering… didn't your grandmother give the heart to your mother when she and your dad got married?" And had Natalie been forced to give it back?

"Oh, my mom and dad were never married," Jasmine tossed off casually as she unzipped her backpack. Then she leaned over and whispered into a stunned Julie's ear, "I was a looooove child. I'm not supposed to know what that means, but I do."

Then, as if the emotional conversation of moments before had never taken place, she started pulling neatly packed clothing from her backpack and hanging it in her closet.

Julie just sat there, her body frozen. Tony hadn't

married Natalie? Tony had gotten a woman pregnant and hadn't married her?

Had he not loved her? Had she been some one-night stand? Had he already been involved with someone else when he found out about the baby?

Memories of Trey intruded—his casual belief that he was entitled to take a lover if he wanted because he was a Davidson, and Davidson men took what they wanted. His sense that he was above having to take responsibility for a bastard child. His total self-involvement, a trait Julie had been completely blind to until it had hit her in the face.

Was she similarly blind about Tony? He seemed to her like the type to be loyal and true, to take responsibility for his mistakes, though she was loath to call Jasmine a mistake. But was she wrong? She'd already caught him in one deception, and though she couldn't specifically remember Tony telling her that he and Natalie had been married, he hadn't gone out of his way to explain the truth either.

Sure, he was a good father now. But how long had it taken him to get to that point? Had he resisted getting tied down? After their condom mishap, when she'd been so freaked out, he'd extolled the virtues of Ethan's mother. He hadn't seemed eager to assume any responsibility.

Tony found her a few minutes later, sitting on Jasmine's bed in a daze as Jasmine continued to hang up her clothes and talk about the planned outing to an amusement park. "Julie, your sister's here."

She shook herself back to the present and stood. She had to get out of there.

"Promise me you'll call me if you need anything," Tony said. "Even if you're mad at me."

All she could think about was escape. She had to think this through before she started blurting out accusations or jumping to conclusions. She ran out of the room, threw on some clothes and fled with Belinda, her heart pounding the entire time.

Chapter Fourteen

"Thanks for coming to get me," Julie said, studying her little sister. Belinda looked a little worse for wear. But *she* wasn't the one who'd been up all night watching the tearoom burn. "Are you okay?"

"Of course not. I'm bummed. Maybe you shouldn't have put my name on the tearoom. Maybe I'm a jinx."

"You're not a jinx. Don't worry, we'll get everything repaired and open back up. I have great insurance." If she wasn't in jail.

Belinda didn't seem that comforted. "You want to drive by and look at it?"

Maybe she should. Maybe it would look better in the daylight.

Belinda turned left onto Jefferson Street. The tearoom looked fine from the outside, except for the plywood over the door and a broken bedroom window. On closer inspection, Julie saw that her new awning was crumpled on one end.

"It's not horrible," Belinda said, parking at the curb.

"Wait till you see the inside."

The yellow tape was gone. In fact, the building appeared to be deserted. Had the investigation released the premises?

Right on cue, her cell phone rang. It was a voice and a name she didn't recognize from the fire marshal's office. "Your building's been released," he said. "We left the keys at the fire station across the street."

"Did you find anything?"

"I can't give you that information, Ma'am."

Damn. That didn't sound good. She repeated the information to Belinda.

"So you're staying here? You don't want to go back to Mom and Dad's?"

"I might as well face it now."

Belinda looked at her sister squarely. "You mean you got me out of bed after five hours' sleep for nothing? If you wanted to go to the tearoom, you could have walked."

"Well, I didn't know they'd let me back in so early. Anyway, why were you up so late?"

"Just, you know, hanging out."

"With Marc?"

"Jules, don't give me the third degree, okay?"

"How old is he? Twenty-three?"

"Twenty-one. When you were my age, you were moving into your own apartment."

True enough. Though Belinda was still in high school, she would be eighteen next month. "I guess you're smart enough to stay out of trouble."

Belinda made the universal groan of a frustrated teenager. "Of course I am!"

With Belinda by her side, Julie was ready to face the damage again. Things looked even worse in the light of day.

Belinda simply stood in the dining room, her mouth hanging open. "Oh, Jules, I'm so sorry."

"Yeah. Me, too." The actual fire damage had been confined to the storeroom and office area, which were a total loss—nothing but the blackened remains of furniture and other items, twisted into unrecognizable lumps. Her computer was a goner, but thankfully she had backed up all of her financial information and she knew it was safe.

Flames hadn't actually reached the dining area, but the firefighters had. They'd pulled down parts of the tin ceiling, and water from the hoses and sprinklers had soaked everything.

The only rooms that remained relatively unscathed were the kitchen and washrooms.

Julie called her insurance company, and an adjuster arrived a short time later. The slight thin-lipped man volunteered little information, walked around making notes on a clipboard and taking pictures. He gave Julie the unwelcome information that she would not receive any compensation until she'd been cleared of any suspicion of arson.

She'd expected as much.

Belinda put her arm around Julie's shoulders. "We can still get started cleaning. That doesn't cost anything. All we need is a bunch of garbage sacks."

"You're right," Julie said, rolling up her figurative sleeves. "We'll do what we can, work with what we have." That had always been her way. A tiny sliver of her old determination surfaced and pushed her into gear.

She raided the cash register, which miraculously was undamaged, and drove to the grocery store to buy trash bags and other cleaning supplies while Belinda started piling up debris.

When Julie returned, she came in through the back door—the only door that still worked—and thought she'd walked into the wrong place.

There was a party going on.

Belinda ran up to her. "Julie, look who came to help!"

It was Tony, plus three helpers—Jasmine, Ethan and Priscilla.

"Jasmine," Julie said, "what about Six Flags?"

"Samantha's got a cold, so she couldn't go with me. But it doesn't matter, 'cause I'd rather help you clean up the mess anyway."

Julie was so touched. These people didn't have anything to gain, but a neighbor had hit some hard times and they simply wanted do what they could. "It's so nice of you to help," she said to them, "but you don't have to…"

"We're helping and that's final," Priscilla said.

Tears came to Julie's eyes. So this was what it was like to have friends, real friends.

With so many helping hands and the use of Tony's wheelbarrow, it didn't take long to haul out the debris. Julie started to make a list of everything she would have to replace, plus some preliminary calculations on what it would cost to repair the walls, floor and ceiling in the damaged areas. She'd learned a lot about building costs during the remodeling.

Linens and curtains were gathered up for a trip to the Laundromat; they might be saved. Tables and chairs were righted, floors swept and mopped, every dish in the place sent through the dishwasher.

By the end of the day, Julie felt a thousand percent better. It didn't look so bad. Once the professional fire-damage people got done, it would look even better. Maybe she wouldn't have to stay closed more than a couple of weeks.

"Who's hungry?" Ethan asked. "I'm thinking the weather's nice enough that we should fire up your grill, Tony."

Tony looked at his watch. "Oh, jeez, I almost forgot. Nat's coming for dinner, and I invited Paolo, too."

"Paolo?" Julie asked.

"Natalie's husband."

"You have your ex and her husband over for dinner?" She couldn't imagine sitting across a table from Trey without her fork ending up in his throat.

"Nat and I get along great. And Paolo—he's terrific. I couldn't ask for a better stepfather for Jasmine."

Julie found Tony's attitude refreshing.

"You girls are coming, right?" Priscilla asked Julie and Belinda.

"Thanks, but I can't," Belinda said. "I have a date. In fact, I really should be gone now."

They all looked at Julie expectantly. "I can't come, either. I've got so much to do. But I really appreciate the invitation."

She could tell her answer didn't sit well with Tony. But he didn't argue. He just looked at her sadly.

They all left except Belinda. "Do you really have anything important to do?" she asked. "Or is something wrong with you and Tony?"

"Things are kind of a mess. He lied to me."

Belinda gasped. "He cheated?"

"Oh, no, nothing like that. But he…well, he wasn't really interested in me. The only reason he slept with me is so he could get me to change my mind about opening the tearoom. He had sex with me so he could get his stupid bar back."

Belinda snorted. "You mean he's faking? I don't think so. Anyway, he must have figured out pretty quick you weren't going to cave, even for him. Yet he didn't run screaming into the night."

Julie recognized the truth in that statement at once. If Tony was only interested in Brady's, why was he still hanging around?

"I guess I need to talk to him," Julie said. "We have to straighten a few things out. But I really do have something important to do."

There was something she'd been neglecting, and now seemed the perfect time to tackle it. She needed to take a hard look at her budget. It had seemed perfectly reasonable when she'd started out, but the actual numbers—both expenses and revenues—had changed so dramatically from her original plan she had no idea where she stood. All she knew was that the balance in the restaurant account wasn't where she'd hoped it would be. Now would be a very good time to make changes, if necessary.

"Maybe I can help," Belinda said when Julie explained her dilemma. She'd apparently forgotten about her date, if she'd had one to begin with.

Together, they analyzed the numbers for almost two hours and then came to a grim conclusion: the tearoom couldn't make a profit, given Julie's current business model.

"André's salary takes too big a bite out of the budget," Julie said. "Not to mention what he's spent on food. The man is insane."

"Can't you keep him on an allowance or something?"

"Oh, it's a moot point. He quit this morning. Took another job."

"Oh. You didn't tell me that."

"With so much else going on, I guess I forgot."

"So hire someone more flexible," Belinda suggested. "And less expensive."

Julie realized she might have to simplify the menu—and cut down on the kitchen help, too.

"As long as you're making changes," Belinda said, "maybe…well, maybe you should think about changing the name."

"Changing the name? Why?"

"Because it's your tearoom. Not mine."

"But you're my inspiration. This place is your legacy. It's going to send you to Princeton. Or Stanford. Or wherever it is you're applying for scholarships this week."

"Yeah. Um, there's something I've been meaning to tell you."

Julie gasped. "Did you get offered a scholarship?"

"Not exactly." Belinda opened her backpack and pulled out a wrinkled piece of paper, handing it reluctantly to Julie. Julie read it top to bottom three times and still didn't get it.

"General Educational Development… What the hell is this?"

"It's a GED certificate."

"I don't understand. You took the GED test?"

"I was bored out of my mind in high school—you knew that. I took the test a few weeks ago. Now I don't have to finish—"

"You're *dropping out?*" Julie shrieked.

Belinda flopped onto a smoke-stained chair. "Don't freak, okay? This is why I've been putting off telling you. I knew you'd be mad. Besides, it's not dropping out if you have a GED. It's like, you know, graduating early."

"But you can't get into a good college with a GED—"

"Well, I could. But I'm not going to college."

Julie felt woozy. She found her way to a chair and sank into it. "Maybe you'd better explain from the beginning."

"I'll go to college someday. But not now. Marc's band got this incredible opportunity. They're going on tour with the Chokers. I'm sure you've heard of them." Belinda nodded encouragingly.

"Actually, no."

Belinda sighed. "They've been on MTV and everything. Well, MTV in Germany. I'm going on tour with him. He might even let me sing a couple of songs. I'm leaving in a week."

Julie had thought there couldn't be any bigger shock to her system than a fire in her tearoom. But this surprise was right up there with an alien invasion. Her sister was a groupie.

"But, Belinda, you're so smart…."

"I'll still go to college. There's time for all that later. Oh, please don't be mad. You've always told me to live life on my terms."

"Yeah, 'cause I thought you wanted to go to college!"

"But I want to live a full life, too."

Julie wanted to argue, but she sensed it was futile. Belinda had that look in her eye that said she was going to do something, and no one would talk her out of it. "Just promise me you'll be careful."

"Sheesh, I'm not stupid."

"What do Mom and Dad say?"

"I had to get their permission to take the GED and they're cool with that, but I haven't told them about going on tour. I think they won't mind, though."

Unfortunately Julie suspected Belinda was right. They'd be happy to get Belinda out from under their roof. One less mouth to feed, though Belinda had been feeding herself pretty well for years.

"I have to go," Belinda said. "We're rehearsing tonight and I promised to bring them pizza." She gave Julie a lightning-fast hug. "Thanks for being understanding. But you should change the name of the tearoom. Maybe another name would give you better luck."

Julie had nothing to say to that. What was happening to the well-ordered life she had visualized when she'd first gotten the idea to open her own tearoom? She would be the captain of her own ship, she'd thought. Master of her universe.

Ha. What a joke. She'd been out of control since the day she'd walked into the dingy bar.

Once again, Julie was alone—just her and her tearoom. How many hours had she spent here in solitude, contemplating the realization of her dream?

Now, in hindsight, she had to ask herself, was running a tearoom all she'd hoped it would be? She had to admit she'd harbored hopes that Trey or someone from his family would come in, and she could rub their noses in it that she was doing just fine without their help, thank you very much.

But none of the Davidsons had cared a whit about her tearoom. And she recognized now how childish and vengeful her motives had been. Given the strange twists her life had taken, she was starting to see what was really important. Friends, family...

And Tony. Where did he fit in?

Though her feelings for Tony ran deep, she'd been careful not to label them. Tony had obviously been disappointed by women in the past, women who'd trifled with his emotions.

She hadn't wanted to be one of those women. She wanted to be straight with him, totally honest, so there would be no misunderstandings.

But then she'd learned of his cold-blooded plan to seduce her into reopening Brady's. On top of that, she'd discovered that Tony hadn't married Jasmine's mother.

But she hadn't bothered to learn the circumstances surrounding either of these matters, had she? She'd simply had a knee-jerk reaction. Tony obviously had a good relationship with Natalie and was a devoted father, and in that respect he was nothing like Trey. And as for the other…she at least ought to listen to what he had to say.

PRISCILLA ANSWERED Tony's door when Julie rang the bell, and she smiled a warm welcome.

"I come bearing gifts." Julie handed Priscilla two white bakery boxes. "Cheesecake and mud pie, saved from the smoke because they were in the fridge. If someone doesn't eat them, they'll just go bad."

"Are you kidding? Around here they won't last fifteen minutes, although I have to say, at the moment the clan is pretty stuffed. Come on in."

As Julie stepped inside, she heard the faint strains of beautifully played guitar music and slightly off-kilter bongo drums. "What's that?"

"That's Paolo. He plays part-time in a mariachi band. I'm not sure where the bongos came from— Ethan or Tony, probably. The girls are taking turns playing them. Come on, we're out on the deck."

The scene that greeted Julie when she stepped through the kitchen door was like something from another era—one of those Elvis beach movies, maybe. A handsome Hispanic man sat on the deck railing, gently strumming his guitar and singing a Mexican ballad. Jasmine, sitting cross-legged on a pillow, tapped softly on the bongo drums.

Everyone else was spread out around the deck, in lawn chairs or pillows, lazy from food and lulled by the music. Dino and an identical spotted pup were sprawled in unmoving heaps, their toys forgotten. Now that the sun was down, sitting outdoors was bearable, even pleasant, with a soft breeze bringing just a hint of cooler weather to come.

It occurred to Julie that this was probably one of those snapshot moments that might never be recreated.

Tony's eyes lit up when he saw her and he smiled. He lay in a hammock that was stretched across one corner of the spacious deck, and he motioned for her to join him.

She shook her head. No, not yet. She still had questions, and cozying up with Tony would only muddle her brain. She sat on a lawn chair near the hammock. Tony was close enough that they could talk softly without others hearing but not so close that they touched.

"He's very good," Julie said.

"Paolo? Yeah. He's even taught Jasmine to play a little bit."

"Sounds like he really is a good stepfather."

"Oh, yeah, the best. Jas is crazy about him."

"How does that make you feel?" Julie asked. Maybe it was a bit forward of her, but she needed to know Tony's views on his role as a parent.

"Truthfully? I feel lucky. Stepparents can be horrible—and believe me, I know. I had four altogether. Out of those four, only one treated me better than a stray dog. So if Jasmine has a stepfather who loves her and spoils her and treats her as his own, I'm happy for her. It just means she has more good influences."

"Do you ever feel jealous?"

He shrugged. "Not really. What I have with Jas is special. No one can take that away."

Julie felt a lump forming in her throat. Yes, she was emotional today, given all that was happening in her life. But the obvious love radiating from Tony was so moving. "You're a really good dad."

"I try, but it isn't easy. The fact her parents live in different houses has never seemed to bother her. But you always wonder if you're somehow unintentionally screwing up your kid's life."

"You and Natalie never married, did you?"

He sat up, looking surprised, probably wondering how she knew. "No, we didn't."

"Jasmine told me this morning. It freaked me out a little."

Tony groaned.

"It doesn't matter to me now," she said quickly, amazed it was true. "What matters is that you're a fantastic father to Jasmine. But I was just surprised. And I wondered why you hadn't mentioned it."

"It just didn't come up." Then he looked down and over Julie's shoulder, anywhere but directly at her. "No, that's not really true. I avoided mentioning it because I didn't think it cast me in a flattering light. The truth is, I wanted to marry Natalie. I assumed, at first, that was the only solution. But her parents were dead set against it. They said if she married me, she was on her own."

Julie was appalled. "She chose her parents over you?"

"Julie, we were sixteen. She was terrified."

"Sixteen!" She tried to imagine Belinda, not much older than that, pregnant and scared. Or even herself at that age. Sixteen was way too young to be married.

"It was good we didn't get married," Tony continued. "Her parents were right. The stress of having a baby is hard enough for adults, much less teenagers. We'd have never made it and we might have ended up hating each other. Instead we have a good relationship, which is good for Jasmine."

"She's a lucky girl."

"No, I'm the lucky one." In that moment, Tony's love for his daughter was so real, so obvious, it was almost a physical presence. And at that same moment, Julie realized she loved Tony. She knew that whatever schemes he'd been involved with, he'd never set out to hurt her. She would be a fool to let him go.

Tony was a person she could rely on. He wasn't going anywhere. He was solid as the building that housed her business and her home—enduring hardships and changes of circumstances but still standing strong.

She'd come so close to losing him by closing her mind, judging and letting the writing on her walls blind her from the truth. In fact, she might still lose him. But how to tell him, after all her waffling and all her flakiness, how she really felt?

Chapter Fifteen

As the evening wound down and little girls' eyes began to droop, tension began to build in Julie's stomach again. Soon she would be alone with Tony. They would have to talk. She would have to tell him her true feelings.

As Paolo packed away his guitar and Kat gathered up the pillows to take them inside, a voice called out, "Hello, is anyone home?"

Priscilla, who'd been lounging on a lawn chair, nursing a glass of wine, sat up so suddenly she spilled wine on her shorts.

The newcomer stood at the fence separating the driveway from the backyard. In the semidarkness Julie saw only the silhouette of a man's head above the fence.

Tony peered suspiciously at the intruder, then abruptly his face relaxed into a smile. "Roark. You just missed the party. Come on back, the gate's open."

As Tony went to greet his new guest halfway,

Julie sidled over to Priscilla. "What do you suppose he's here for?" she asked, fear making her voice shrill.

"Don't panic," Priscilla said. "I don't think he's here to haul you off to jail. He doesn't normally do the arresting. He may just be here to play shuffle-board or something."

But Julie didn't think so. Even as he shook hands with Tony and went through some sort of male-bonding trade of punches, his gaze sought out Julie.

Or maybe Priscilla. But if he was trying to catch Priscilla's eye, it was hopeless. The normally poised woman was frantically trying to get the red wine spot off her shorts with a damp paper towel.

Priscilla cursed in the dainty way only she could. "I've got to go soak these shorts before the stain sets in," she said, making a hasty escape before Epperson even reached the deck.

Julie just stood there, feeling like a sitting duck. She wanted to run and hide from whatever news he was about to give her—and surely that's why he was here, because he was coming right toward her.

"Ms. Polk."

"You're looking for me?"

"I tried you on your cell phone, but I kept getting voice mail."

Because the battery was dead and the charger burned up. "But still you found me," she said cautiously.

"The Dallas Fire Rescue grapevine is alive and

well. Someone on the A shift at Station 59 saw you headed this way."

Sometimes Julie wondered if the firefighters had anything better to do than watch her comings and goings.

"I wanted to see you face-to-face anyway," the investigator said, turning serious, and Julie felt a little shaky in the knees. She steadied herself against Tony, who'd moved to stand protectively by her side. Ethan, too, had stopped to greet Epperson and listen to whatever he had to say.

The air was charged with tension.

Then suddenly the man smiled. "Would you all stop looking at me like I'm an executioner? I've got good news. The official report will be filed tomorrow morning, but since I've put you through hell, I thought it was only fair to let you know now. I've made my official determination of the cause of the fire, and it's not arson. Apparently a nail went through an old wire during your remodeling and caused a short. It was probably smoldering there inside your wall for weeks."

Julie nearly passed out with relief. "So does this mean…?" She could hardly grasp it.

"You're off the hook. You should be able to collect on your insurance and rebuild in no time."

She wanted to throw herself at Roark Epperson and hug him, but she settled for a handshake. "Thank you. You have no idea how happy you've just made me."

"Hey, Roark," Ethan said, "We've got the old

shuffleboard table set up and ready to go. Seems you owe me a rematch."

"No kidding? Got some warm beer to go with it?"

Ethan grinned. "Would you settle for a cold one?"

As the two men stepped inside, Tony pulled Julie into a bear hug. "This is great! Everything's going your way now, I can feel it. Hey, you want to stay and play shuffleboard?"

"I really need to get home and get some sleep. Long day tomorrow. You're not working tomorrow, right?"

Tony shook his head.

"Come over in the morning. I'll fix you some breakfast—I've got lots of eggs to use up. And we can talk."

Tony immediately sobered. "Oh. You know, for a minute there, I forgot how bad I screwed up."

"Maybe not so bad. We'll get everything straightened out tomorrow, okay?"

"Anyplace, anytime you say, babe."

THE NEXT MORNING, bright and early, Julie was on the phone with the contractor who'd done her original remodeling. "You've got to fit me in, Sid," she insisted. "Every day I stay closed is another day closer to bankruptcy."

"You want I should get no sleep?" he asked, but she knew he would take the job. He loved to complain, but she sensed he would come through.

"Sid, someone's knocking at the door. I'll call you back." Let him think about it. She went to the tearoom's battered door, which Ethan had rigged to at least open, close and lock. Although she and Tony hadn't set a particular time to meet, she thought that was who she'd find.

She wanted to pour out all her doubts and worries, her mixed feelings about her future, and she knew without guessing at all that he would fold her into his arms and reassure her that everything would be okay. Belinda was a smart kid, he would say. She's entitled to follow her heart and maybe make some mistakes. She'll come out okay. The important thing was that she lived her life on her own terms, just as Julie wanted to do.

He would have ideas about how to fix her finances, too. He would remind her that he could float her a loan if she needed one. He would volunteer free labor—his and that of all his friends, whether they agreed or not.

So she was disappointed when it wasn't Tony standing on the sidewalk but Eloisa and Josephina.

Surprised though she was, she managed a smile for the other woman. "Eloisa! Come on in. I was about to put some coffee on."

"I do coffee," Eloisa said eagerly.

"You don't have to—" Julie tried to object, but Eloisa seemed not to hear. She made a beeline for the kitchen, and Julie followed her with a shrug.

"I know the kitchen good," Eloisa said. And, sure enough, she did brew a pot of coffee without any instruction from Julie. "I work in kitchen in Acapulco."

"Eloisa, if you're wondering about your job, you'll still have it when I reopen the restaurant. But that won't be for weeks yet. Three weeks, maybe more. You understand?"

"Yes, you give me job."

"In a few weeks."

Eloisa nodded. "But I work in kitchen, yes?"

"You want to be a sous chef?" Julie asked incredulously.

"Sous chef. That's chef's helper?"

"Right. An assistant chef." And in a kitchen serving the kind of gourmet food Belinda's did, it was a highly skilled position.

"No. I want to be top chef. André, he is mean and greedy. I do his job. A lot better and cheaper."

Julie resisted the urge to giggle. Eloisa, her head chef?

"I can cook," Eloisa said stubbornly.

"I'm sure you can." She could probably make great Tex-Mex food. But Belinda's was not a Mexican restaurant.

Eloisa shrugged. "I show you." And she proceeded, over Julie's fading objections, to cook up a delectable and innovative omelet with prosciutto, green onions and cream cheese. Not only was the food delicious, but Eloisa had produced it in less than five minutes, wielding her utensils with the ease of a practiced chef.

Julie, who held Josephina while Eloisa worked, was almost afraid to ask. "What else can you cook?"

"Anything. Lamb, chicken, uh…" She struggled for the word. "SpaghettiOs?"

"Pasta."

"Yes, pasta. Enchiladas so good you cry."

"Are you trained? Did you go to school?"

"School? To cook?" She dismissed that as foolishness. "I learn from Mama. And I watch Emeril on the TV."

Suddenly an idea struck Julie—a terrible, wonderful idea. It was crazy. It went against almost everything she'd fought for all these weeks and months. But it made a kooky kind of sense.

She'd already decided she needed a different kind of chef and a simpler menu. Why not a casual tearoom by day? Fewer tables. Fewer staff. A shorter, simplified menu but still classy and appealing to women.

A bar by night. A nice bar, a friendly neighborhood place. Clean. Inviting. Burgers and cold beer. Darts and shuffleboard. No smoking.

Brady's Tavern and Tearoom.

Now that she knew and understood this neighborhood better, she could see that it would fit right in. More upscale than the old Brady's, certainly, but not off-putting. Friendlier and less expensive than Belinda's. People could bring their kids. Men could order a burger.

"Ms. Julie?" Eloisa said. "What you think?"

"I think you're hired."

Eloisa dropped her spatula and threw her arms around Julie with a squeal.

The more Julie thought about it, the more she realized the answer had been in front of her all along if only she hadn't been so pigheaded. There'd been no need to choose between a bar and a tearoom. She could do both and double her profits.

She couldn't wait to tell Tony.

Tony. She loved him—oh, how she loved him. She'd gone to sleep last night sure of it and woken up this morning even more positive. But she'd taken his affections for granted. She'd been so ridiculously focused on her life, her problems, she hadn't given much thought to how all this was affecting Tony.

That was all going to change.

She promised Eloisa she would be in touch soon. They would have to work out a menu, which would be a whole new challenge, given the language barrier. Then, once she was alone again, she made plans—not plans for the new Brady's but plans for her and Tony. From this moment forward, Tony would be a part of all her plans.

If he would have her.

Unwilling to live with the suspense a moment longer, she picked up her cell and dialed Tony's number. She didn't care if she woke him up.

But no one answered.

Disappointed, she looked out the window—and there he was, striding with determination across the street toward her. She walked outside to wave a welcome, and he quickened his pace. He didn't stop until he was nose to nose with her.

"You just have to know one thing," he said. "I love you."

She took a step back in pure self-defense. If she didn't, she was going to be all over him. The smell of him made her think about sex—and she didn't think that should be her first priority.

"Oh, Tony." She tried not to cry. She had things to say. "You were right all along. Belinda's Tearoom was wrong for this neighborhood. A few blocks north in Kessler Park or even in Bishop Arts, maybe I could have made it. But not on Jefferson Street. Even if it hadn't been for the fire, I would have been broke in another few weeks." It was easier to start with the less personal stuff, she decided.

"You're giving up?" He looked like a kid who'd just been told Santa Claus is a myth.

"No. That's the good part. I've decided to reopen Brady's, but with a slight twist—Brady's Tavern and Tearoom. Eloisa's going to cook for me. I'm going to serve hamburgers."

Tony's eyes widened. "And ribs?"

"If you think it's a good idea." She shuddered a little at the thought. But her idea hadn't worked. She needed to listen to other people for a change. "The tearoom was sort of snobby, wasn't it?"

"That's not the word I would have used." But he said it cautiously.

"My mother said I was putting on airs. I was trying to prove something to Trey and his family, to be someone I wasn't."

Tony adjusted the collar of her shirt. "You were doing something that made you happy, honey.

You're entitled to live your dream any way you see fit."

"But it wouldn't have made me happy. It was one big headache. And when Trey and his family completely ignored me, I realized at least half the reason I had for opening a tearoom was bogus. Shallow."

"So what would make you happy?"

"I just want to belong somewhere. To be part of something that's bigger than me. I want some control over my life. But if I ever had any control over anything, it was just an illusion. My restaurant burned down, my sister is running off with a rock musician and on top of everything else..."

The words stuck in her throat.

He smoothed a strand of hair off her forehead. Oh, the feel of his touch. It would be so easy to fall into it, to let hormones rule.

"On top of everything else, I love you," Tony said again. "Or did you not hear me the first time?"

Julie was staring at him, her lips slightly parted, her chest rising and falling in rapid succession. He had no idea what she was thinking. Was she shocked? Horrified? He'd told her the unvarnished truth this time. He'd wanted no more deception between them.

"You can pretend I didn't. It sorta slipped out. Priscilla says I fall in love too easy. And maybe I do. But this time I know it's for real. And for keeps."

She continued to watch him with unnerving intensity.

He felt compelled to fill the silence. In direct opposition to his self-preservation instincts, he continued to blather. "I'm not even sure I know what love is. But I know I think about you all the time. And I worry about you, about whether you're happy, whether you're safe. And sometimes I just want to hold you."

That, he realized, was something new. He'd felt lust for plenty of women. But this tenderness? The tightness in his throat when he thought about losing Julie? He'd never known those feelings before. Was that love?

"I love you, too, Tony."

"You…you do?"

"Uh-huh."

"Don't you want to know about what Bing said?"

"It doesn't matter anymore."

"I want to tell you what happened anyway." He had to get it off his chest. "I didn't want anything to do with any plan to sweet-talk you into reopening Brady's. Until I saw you. Just the way you walked out the door of Brady's, your head held high, so full of purpose, your hair all shiny and gold…" He paused, looking off into space, a slight smile on his lips. "I wasn't willing to let anyone else have the job."

"So you had an ulterior motive."

"Yeah. Even if I hadn't, Julie, I'd have been at your door every day anyway. But over the next few weeks I saw how excited you were about the tearoom, how much you loved decorating every little corner and working out the menu and choosing your dishes and sewing those curtains, night after night. And you know what I realized?"

"That I was stubborn as a squirrel trying to get at the bird feeder?"

"No. I realized you had a right to follow your dream. Because it was making you happy. And being happy is a lot more important than making a ton of money—or catering to a bunch of cranky firefighters.

"If my only goal had been to change your mind about the tearoom, I'd have given up. But I was crazy about you from the very first day. It wasn't like I was faking anything, ever."

Julie felt the first pinpricks of guilt. He'd been crazy about her, and she'd treated him as an afterthought. Though she'd seen the potential, she hadn't felt she could invest everything in a relationship. Not when the last one had gone so badly.

"I guess the joke was on me," he said. "I didn't want my heart to get stomped on again and I swore I wouldn't fall in love with you. But I did."

Tony backed Julie up against the tearoom door, much as he had just before their first kiss. "So that's it. The last of the deep, dark secrets."

Julie sighed. "Is this the part where we get to kiss and make up?"

"If you insist."

He closed his mouth over hers, and his kiss was every bit as exciting as the very first one had been.

Unfortunately they had an audience. Applause, whistles and catcalls broke out from across the street, where most of the B shift was standing around in Station 59's driveway.

"Would you guys get lives?" Tony called out. Then he opened the door, nudged Julie inside and closed it again. "I really want to get naked with you."

"I can't. The contractor's on his way over here right now. But, Tony, I swear I'll never make this business a priority over you again. People are what matter. While I was busy obsessing over account balances, Belinda was off falling in love, and she never even told me. It's all going to change."

He caressed her face. "Don't worry about me. All I've ever wanted is the same thing you want. To belong. I don't think either of us were born into an ideal family. But look how lucky we are now. We get to make our own family. You, me, Jasmine."

Jasmine. Julie lightly touched the silver heart, still in her pocket. How had the girl known?

Julie wanted to say more. But her heart was stuck in her throat, preventing any words from emerging. She couldn't believe Tony was so understanding about everything, so willing to accept her, quirks and mood swings and all.

"So what do you say? I'm not a millionaire and I don't own any fancy department stores, but I'll love you more than any ten millionaires could. Let's get married."

"What?"

He grinned. "Priscilla would kill me right now, but I don't care. Let's get married."

There, he'd said it again. She wasn't hearing things. "Priscilla told me this would happen, you know. She warned me not to hurt you."

"You're not going to, are you?"

She shook her head. "I don't think so."

"I'm looking for a yes or a no here," he said.

"Yes." It was the easiest answer in the world.

JULIE'S INSURANCE company came through with a check almost instantly, and it was far more than she'd thought she would get. The cleanup and renovations to Brady's Tavern and Tearoom were moving along with amazing speed. Her beautiful wood bar, which she'd feared was damaged beyond repair, underwent a miraculous transformation. Laundering and pressing restored her curtains. And the professional cleaners got rid of the last of the smoke smell.

She set a date for reopening.

About half of her previous staff wanted to come back—which worked out perfectly. She hired Alonzo, formerly her uncle Brady's right-hand man, to manage the bar, which would now include a limited menu of burgers and barbecue, along with some mini quiches and stuffed mushrooms for the female diners.

It all fell together so easily, so beautifully, she wondered why she'd ever resisted this idea.

Belinda sent her postcards from the road. It still terrified Julie to think of her baby sister out in the big, bad world, but she sounded remarkably content and unnervingly adult.

It was a few days before the reopening—she refused to call it a grand opening this time, for fear of jinxing herself—and Julie was touching up the paint.

It still looked like her tearoom—but friendlier now. She'd gotten rid of the fussy table linens in favor of white butcher paper. The stuffy paintings she'd originally bought for the walls had been smoke- and water-damaged beyond repair, so she'd replaced them with artwork from Oak Cliff artisans, all of it offered for sale; yet another revenue stream, and as the paintings sold, the decor would change continually.

Tony was mysteriously absent. He'd spent almost every minute he wasn't on duty with her, helping her get ready to reopen. So his absence was noted—but not worried about. He liked to surprise her, and she liked to let him. Before, he'd held back a little, worried about overwhelming her with affection and scaring her off, as he had other girlfriends.

Now he just let it fly, and she lapped it up. She'd never felt so honored, so cherished, so loved without reservation. Her whole life was coming together like a jigsaw puzzle of the most beautiful, perfect sunrise.

Now she heard a noise at the door, and her whole being grew brighter as Tony entered, a big, dirt-eating grin on his face. But then he got a better look at what she was doing and frowned disapprovingly. He loped across the tearoom toward her.

"What are you doing on that ladder and not even holding on to anything? Jeez, the first time I met you you were falling off a ladder, and don't think I've forgotten. I told you I'd do the hard stuff." He steadied the ladder and held a hand out to help her down.

"Tony, I'm only on the second step." But she loved that he was protective. He'd made her promise to slap him down if he got carried away, but so far it didn't bother her a bit.

To humor him, she stepped off the ladder and laid aside her paintbrush. "Where've you been?"

His grin returned. "Wait until you see. You're going to take back every mean thing you ever thought about cops and firefighters." He ran back to the door and opened it. "Okay, guys," he yelled. "Bring it in."

Julie stared, slack-jawed, as Brady's antique shuffleboard table came in through the door. Close on its heels was the dartboard. Then several neon signs. And finally in came Sir Edward, the wooden cigar-store Indian.

Tony, directing the placement of each item carted in by at least a dozen off-duty firefighters and cops, kept glancing at Julie to see if she would object. But she was too amazed to do anything but stare. She'd been regretting her headstrong decision to sell all the quirky things that had made the old Brady's what it was, but she hadn't imagined there'd be any way to get them back.

Tony had managed it.

He joined her, sliding an arm around her waist. "You're not saying much."

"I'm in shock. How did you buy all this stuff back?"

"I didn't. They're giving it to you as a sort of housewarming gift for the new Brady's."

"And they were feeling a little guilty for ripping me off," she concluded.

"Yeah. That, too."

When the naked-lady picture came through the door, she finally shook her head. "I can't put *that* back up. This is a family establishment."

"How about in the men's restroom?" Tony cajoled. "She *is* a part of Brady's history."

She threw up her hands. "Fine. I'll drape her with scarves."

Tony laughed. "Brady would think that was hilarious."

It was funny, Julie agreed. This was going to be one funky tearoom.

But it was going to work. Somehow this strange amalgam of good taste and tacky honky-tonk nostalgia was going to work. It was a reflection of Oak Cliff itself—the old and the new, rich and poor, tasteful and tacky living cheek by jowl, each element becoming greater for being part of the whole.

Just as she was a more whole, more complete person for having moved here, for having fallen in love with a true hero.

She gave Tony an extra squeeze. "How would

you feel about having our wedding here? All my dreams in one place."

He grinned down at her. "Perfect."

* * * * *

Watch for Priscilla's story,
An Honorable Man, the final story in the
FIREHOUSE 59 *series,*
available March 2007,
only from Harlequin American Romance

Happily ever after is just the beginning...

Turn the page for a sneak preview of
A HEARTBEAT AWAY
by
Eleanor Jones

Harlequin Everlasting—Every great love
has a story to tell.™
A brand-new series from Harlequin Books

Special? A prickle ran down my neck and my heart started to beat in my ears. Was today really special?

"Tuck in," he ordered.

I turned my attention to the feast that he had spread out on the ground. Thick, home-cooked-ham sandwiches, sausage rolls fresh from the oven and a huge variety of mouthwatering scones and pastries. Hunger pangs took over, and I closed my eyes and bit into soft homemade bread.

When we were finally finished, I lay back against the bluebells with a groan, clutching my stomach.

Daniel laughed. "Your eyes are bigger than your stomach," he told me.

I leaned across to deliver a punch to his arm, but he rolled away, and when my fist met fresh air I collapsed in a fit of giggles before relaxing on my back and staring up into the flawless blue sky. We lay like that for quite a while, Daniel and I, side by side in companionable silence, until he stretched out his hand in an arc that encompassed the whole area.

"Don't you think that this is the most beautiful place in the entire world?"

His voice held a passion that echoed my own feelings, and I rose onto my elbow and picked a buttercup to hide the emotion that clogged my throat.

"Roll over onto your back," I urged, prodding him with my forefinger. He obliged with a broad grin, and I reached across to place the yellow flower beneath his chin.

"Now, let us see if you like butter."

When a yellow light shone on the tanned skin below his jaw, I laughed.

"There…you do."

For an instant our eyes met and I had the strangest sense that I was drowning in those honey-brown depths. The scent of bluebells engulfed me. A roaring filled my ears, and then unexpectedly, in one smooth movement Daniel rolled me onto my back and plucked a buttercup of his own.

"And do *you* like butter, Lucy McTavish?" he asked. When he placed the flower against my skin, time stood still.

His long lean body was suspended over mine, pinning me against the grass. Daniel…dear, comfortable, familiar Daniel was suddenly bringing out in me the strangest sensations.

"Do you, Lucy McTavish?" he asked again, his voice low and vibrant.

My eyes flickered toward his, the whisper of a

sigh escaped my lips and although a strange lethargy had crept into my limbs, I somehow felt as if all my nerve endings were on fire. He felt it, too—I could see it in his warm brown eyes. And when he lowered his face to mine, it seemed to me the most natural thing in the world.

None of the kisses I had ever experienced could have even begun to prepare me for the feel of Daniel's lips on mine. My entire body floated on a tide of ecstasy that shut out everything but his soft, warm mouth, and I knew that this was what I had been waiting for the whole of my life.

"Oh, Lucy." He pulled away to look into my eyes. "Why haven't we done this before?"

Holding his gaze, I gently touched his cheek, then I curled my fingers through the short thick hair at the base of his skull, overwhelmed by the longing to drown again in the sensations that flooded our bodies. And when his long tanned fingers crept across my tingling skin, I knew I could deny him nothing.

* * * * *

Be sure to look for
A HEARTBEAT AWAY,
available February 27, 2007.
And look, too, for
THE DEPTH OF LOVE
by Margot Early,
the story of a couple who must learn
that love comes in many guises—
and in the end it's the only thing that counts.

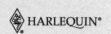

EVERLASTING LOVE™

Every great love has a story to tell™

Save $1.⁰⁰ off

the purchase of
any Harlequin
Everlasting Love novel

Coupon valid from January 1, 2007
until April 30, 2007.

Valid at retail outlets in the U.S. only.
Limit one coupon per customer.

5 65373 00076 2 (8100)0 11302

HEUSCPN0407

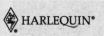

EVERLASTING LOVE™

Every great love has a story to tell™

Save $1.⁰⁰ off

**the purchase of
any Harlequin
Everlasting Love novel**

Coupon valid from January 1, 2007
until April 30, 2007.

Valid at retail outlets in Canada only.
Limit one coupon per customer.

52607370

HECDNCPN0407

The real action happens behind the scenes!

Introducing

SECRET LIVES OF DAYTIME DIVAS,

a new miniseries from author

SARAH MAYBERRY

TAKE ON ME

Dylan Anderson was the cause of Sadie Post's biggest humiliation. Now that he's back, she's going to get a little revenge. But no one ever told her that revenge could be this sweet...and oh, so satisfying.

Available March 2007

Don't miss the other books in the SECRET LIVES OF DAYTIME DIVAS miniseries!

Look for *All Over You* in April 2007
and *Hot for Him* in May 2007.

Silhouette®
Romantic
SUSPENSE

Excitement, danger and passion guaranteed!

Same great authors and riveting editorial
you've come to know and love
from Silhouette Intimate Moments.

> *New York Times*
> bestselling author
> Beverly Barton
> is back with the
> latest installment
> in her popular
> miniseries,
> The Protectors.
> HIS ONLY
> OBSESSION
> is available
> next month from
> Silhouette®
> Romantic Suspense

Look for it wherever you buy books!

REQUEST YOUR FREE BOOKS!
2 FREE NOVELS PLUS 2
FREE GIFTS!

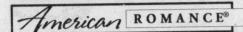

American | **ROMANCE**®

Heart, Home & Happiness!

YES! Please send me 2 FREE Harlequin American Romance® novels and my 2 FREE gifts. After receiving them, if I don't wish to receive any more books, I can return the shipping statement marked "cancel." If I don't cancel, I will receive 4 brand-new novels every month and be billed just $4.24 per book in the U.S., or $4.99 per book in Canada, plus 25¢ shipping and handling per book and applicable taxes, if any*. That's a savings of close to 15% off the cover price! I understand that accepting the 2 free books and gifts places me under no obligation to buy anything. I can always return a shipment and cancel at any time. Even if I never buy another book from Harlequin, the two free books and gifts are mine to keep forever.

154 HDN EEZK   354 HDN EEZV

Name _____ (PLEASE PRINT)

Address _____ Apt. #

City _____ State/Prov. _____ Zip/Postal Code

Signature (if under 18, a parent or guardian must sign)

Mail to the **Harlequin Reader Service**®:
IN U.S.A.: P.O. Box 1867, Buffalo, NY 14240-1867
IN CANADA: P.O. Box 609, Fort Erie, Ontario L2A 5X3

Not valid to current Harlequin American Romance subscribers.

Want to try two free books from another line?
Call 1-800-873-8635 or visit www.morefreebooks.com.

* Terms and prices subject to change without notice. NY residents add applicable sales tax. Canadian residents will be charged applicable provincial taxes and GST. This offer is limited to one order per household. All orders subject to approval. Credit or debit balances in a customer's account(s) may be offset by any other outstanding balance owed by or to the customer. Please allow 4 to 6 weeks for delivery.

Your Privacy: Harlequin is committed to protecting your privacy. Our Privacy Policy is available online at www.eHarlequin.com or upon request from the Reader Service. From time to time we make our lists of customers available to reputable firms who may have a product or service of interest to you. If you would prefer we not share your name and address, please check here. ☐

HAR07

This February...

Catch NASCAR Superstar **Carl Edwards** *in*

SPEED DATING!

Kendall assesses risk for a living—so she's the last person you'd expect to see on the arm of a race-car driver who thrives on the unpredictable. But when a bizarre turn of events—and NASCAR hotshot Dylan Hargreave—inspire her to trade in her ever-so-structured existence for "life in the fast lane" she starts to feel she might be on to something!

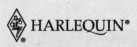

HARLEQUIN®

American ROMANCE®

COMING NEXT MONTH

#1153 HER SECRET SONS by Tina Leonard
The Tulips Saloon
Pepper Forrester has a secret—make that two secrets. Thirteen years ago she became pregnant with Luke McGarrett's twin boys and, knowing him as she did, didn't tell him he was a father. With both of them living in Tulips again, the time has come to confess. All looks to be well, until history begins to repeat itself....

#1154 AN HONORABLE MAN by Kara Lennox
Firehouse 59
Priscilla Garner doesn't want a man, nor does she need one. She's more interested in being accepted as the only female firefighter at Station 59. But when she needs a date—platonic, of course—for her cousin's wedding, she turns to one-time fling Roark Epperson. He knows she's not looking for long-term, but that doesn't mean he isn't planning on changing her mind!

#1155 SOMEWHERE DOWN IN TEXAS by Ann DeFee
Marci Hamilton loves her hometown of Port Serenity, but life's been a little dull lately. So she enters a barbecue sauce cook-off with events held all over Texas. Although it's sponsored by country music superstar J. W. Watson, Marci wouldn't recognize him—or any singer other than Willie Nelson. So when a handsome cowboy comes to her aid, she has no idea it's J.W. himself....

#1156 A SMALL-TOWN GIRL by Shelley Galloway
Still stung from her former partner's rejection, Genevieve Slate joins the police department in sleepy Lane's End hoping for a fresh start and a slower pace of life. But a sexy math teacher named Cary Hudson, a couple of crazed beagles and a town beset by basketball fever mean there's no rest in store for this small-town cop!

www.eHarlequin.com

HARCNM0207